The Last Girls On Earth

HAYLEY ANDERTON

This book is dedicated to every single Wattpad reader who read Silence. You gave me confidence as a writer, hope as an author, and your love as readers. It was the beginning of everything, and it brought this story into the world. Thank you for everything.

OTHER BOOKS BY HAYLEY ANDERTON

All books are available to purchase as paperbacks or ebooks. All books are also enrolled in Kindle Unlimited.

Apocalypse Series

Book 1: Apocalypse
Book 2: Fallout
Book 3: Chaos
Book 4: Sacrifice

Coming Soon...
The Risen Series

Book 1: The Risen
Book 2: The Lost
Book 3: The Remains

Other Books:

Double Bluff

You are a doll in the Devil's hand
He crushes your soul to sand
No God shall ever hear you cry
You were only ever born to die.

RAVEN

It's a year today since Ma jumped from twenty-one stories up.
When I close my eyes, I still see her falling. I see myself
leaning out of the open window, grasping at thin air as
though I can catch her before she hits the ground.
Sometimes, when I'm dreaming, I imagine that I'm her, and I
feel my heart lurch up in my chest at the feeling of falling. I
wake up crying for help, but she didn't scream as she
dropped. I guess she was looking for some relief from this
life that she knew would never come.

I only hope that she found it.

It's quiet at home now. Without her humming cheery
tunes throughout the day, or finding ways to make us all
laugh, these walls only hold silence and misery. I stand in our
single room, thinking of her, rooted to the spot where I
stood a year ago by the ache of her absence. When she was
here, there was always something to live for. Now, it's getting
harder to find reasons to keep fighting.

My only reason is Jonah. He's still asleep, curled up in the
hollow in the wall. He's not particularly well hidden, with
only a translucent curtain covering his sleeping body. If we
get a surprise check, we'll all be killed. My brother wasn't
meant to be born. One child per family, that's the rule. No

one has an immediate family bigger than three. Even us, since Mum died. But his birth seven years ago gave the government the right to end every life in this household if they ever found out. They'd likely do it with pleasure, too. Three less ration cards to accommodate for. A single room left unoccupied so someone else can move in off the streets. The living crisis in this country has been spiraling out of control since long before I was born, and I've watched the world around me crumble along the way. Now, we're all suffering through a nightmare where people like us have nothing, and there's no way to crawl out of the hole we have been forced to burrow into.

But I have to keep life moving. There's nothing gained by standing still. We eat, sleep, suffer, repeat, and that's on a good day. If we stop to wonder why we even bother, we might stop entirely. I guess that's why Ma isn't here today.

It's time to head out. I don't have a way to tell the time – not until I get into the square and look at the clock - but I know I'm up late. Sunlight's streaming through the crack in our shabby cloth curtain. It'll be harder to navigate the market at this time of day – it'll be packed. But today of all days, I can afford to cut myself some slack. The pain of Ma's loss is too harsh today to beat myself up even further. Besides, I've got nothing better to do than peruse the stalls that I can't afford. I may as well take my time.

I hurtle down the stairs, feeling dizzy as I spiral round and round. It's been a few days since my last proper meal and my body has noticed. The front door to the block of apartments hangs off its hinges. Someone broke in last week, and no one's bothered to put the door back in place. There's no point since there's nothing in here to take. If anything, the person who broke in probably just wanted somewhere to shelter from the rain. We all protect what little possessions we have, but no one would ever deny someone a square of tile above their head.

It's bright outside today. I can see the rays of sun peeking over the high-rise buildings, even if I can't feel them much.

There are a couple of kids tossing around a ball made of rags in the crowded street. The rags fly over the heads of strangers, and the children giggle. I fumble in my pocket for a rusty penny and toss it to them. They scrabble for it like a pack of dogs. It won't buy them anything; they'd have to collect hundreds just to buy a loaf of bread and some butter. But maybe they can toss it for entertainment.

I lose myself in the crush of people. I keep tight hold of the money and ration cards in my pocket. There are plenty of thieves around. I should know. I've done my fair share of stealing. But not today. I don't have the energy to even try to steal, and for once, I have enough money for a little food. I guess Pa didn't drink all our money away this week.

I reach the market square where all of the stalls and carts are set up. I follow the flow of the crowd, shuffling past stalls offering the luxury items I can't afford. For those with extra coins to spare, there is a medicine stall, a van selling clothes and shoes, and a second-hand book stall. I don't like to linger long, knowing I'll never be able to own things so precious and expensive. Most of the crowd pushes on, heading toward the stalls selling absolute necessities.

I hit the food carts – the fishmonger, the grocery cart, and the baker's van. The queues are always long here, so I get in line to buy a loaf of bread. I swallow a lump in my throat as I shuffle forward. Before Ma got the job singing uptown, she worked for the baker's van.

I get a proper look at it from the front of the line. It looks the same way it always has; leaning to the left on one wheel, the tin exterior rusted from the rain. Years ago, I would have walked past and seen Mum inside, kneading the gritty brown dough with flour smudged across her face. She'd always smile at me on my way to the market. Sometimes, she would pretend she didn't know who I was, a little game to keep me entertained as we roleplayed as the customer and the server, even when I had no money. Sometimes her boss would let me 'sample' the bread, and I wouldn't spend the morning hungry.

But this morning, he doesn't even look me in the eye when I pass him my ration card and coins for my weekly loaf. He doesn't owe me anything anymore. Maybe he doesn't even remember me.

The town's still busy – the clock looming over the marketplace tells me that it's half nine. I'm not as late as I thought, but the marketplace is still more crowded than usual. The air is thick with suffocating smoke snaking from the tops of buildings and from the few cars that sputter and spit oil as they weave through the busy streets. It clings to my lungs, making me cough. Around me, other's splutter too, hacking tar-like liquid into spoiled handkerchiefs. It makes me feel sick, and suddenly, I just want to hurry home. I use the last of my money to buy some vegetables for a broth, wishing I could take more home for Jonah and me. But that's all I can get with the money Pa gave to me and the rations we're allowed. It'll have to do.

But I have plenty of time. The thing about having no purpose in life is that time is something you can spend in abundance. I have no job to get to or extracurriculars like the kids uptown. The only thing to do is to hang around and wait for something to happen.

Wren is working hard as I approach the meat vendor's van. There's a big slab of steak on the counter which she's chopping up into small slices. It's making my mouth water. I haven't tasted meat in over a year now. When Ma was alive and working, we were able to afford such luxuries on occasion, but now, it would cost everything we have for a small piece of steak. We'd eat like kings for a night and then starve like peasants.

Wren packages a slice of the meat for someone and hands it over, taking a moment to wipe her brow. Her short black hair clings to her sweet round face in thin tendrils, the product of a hard day's labor. Her family have owned this business for generations, ever since her great-grandmother moved from Vietnam as a chef before Britain closed the borders entirely. Now, Wren is following in her footsteps in what's left of the culinary industry. I envy her. I envy her having something to do with herself.

She spots me and waves with a toothy grin. Her eyes are such a dark brown that they're almost black, but her smile always brings a sparkle to her gaze. I smile as I head over to greet her.

"Hey! Fancy seeing you here," she says brightly, as though we don't have this same conversation every day.

"Hey, Wren. Been busy today?"

"It's been non-stop! I guess it must be pay day. I've got sores on my hands." She pauses to smile at me. "How's things?" Her face falls once again. "Oh God, I can't believe I just asked that. I know what today is...I'm so sorry, Raven."

I force a smile and a shrug. There's no use in dwelling on what can't be changed. Besides, I know that Wren doesn't have a mean bone in her body. "It's okay."

"No, Raven, it's not. I'm an idiot. I always say the wrong thing. Here, come around the back. My Pa can handle the customers for a minute."

She steps down out of the van and ushers me to follow her behind it. We cram in the space between the vehicle and the building behind it. She hugs me tight and I feel a lump in my throat. Somehow, her kindness is making it harder to cope.

"Don't look now but I've slipped something into your pocket," she whispers as she holds me close. "I made you a care package...I didn't forget about today, I promise. Don't look until you're home. I don't want either of us getting in trouble."

I can barely speak. I know what will be in the package - extra food. It's strictly forbidden to take more than your own ration card allows. Wren must have taken food from the butcher's van or off her own table to feed me. Though I know her family are better off than most and that she won't go hungry because of this, she could've lost everything by helping me. Her kindness never ceases to amaze me.

"Wren...thank you. Thank you so much."

"Don't mention it," she says as she pulls away. She taps her finger on my nose affectionately. "Seriously. Don't."

I can't help smiling. Wren always knows how to bring out the best in me. Even in this cruel world, she manages to find ways to raise a smile from everyone. She's the same with her customers. It's people like her that make this life a little easier to live.

She glances up at the van.

"I'd better get back to work. But Raven...you know where to find me if you need me. I'll see you tomorrow, yeah?"

"Tomorrow," I say. Because I've got nowhere else to be. Neither does Wren. None of us do. This is our life.

The package in my jacket pocket feels heavy as I rush home with the rest of my groceries. I'm paranoid about getting caught, like the days when I walk home with stolen goods in my pockets. I'm not proud of doing things I shouldn't, but not many people know the reason I steal. It's not out of greed. I don't do it for me. I'd risk everything for Jonah, to keep his stomach lined even when he's not meant to exist. Now that Mum is gone, I have to be the one to keep us afloat.

I'm weary by the time I get back to our building, though I've barely been awake an hour. I've always tried to stay healthy – back when I knew Logan, he'd teach me to box and we would race near his home where the streets were clearer. But now I just don't have the energy. There's nothing less appealing than a run when you've barely eaten all week. Tiredness and hunger are more like emotions than sensations, and they run you into the ground.

Jonah's awake when I get home, exhausted from climbing the stairs. As usual, it strikes me how unwell he looks. His skin is yellowed from lack of sun and his curls always seem damp with sweat, like he's running a fever. He can't go outside – not if he wants to live. He's unregistered, and if he was spotted by government officials, if he was asked to show his identification, he wouldn't be able to. He would be carted off and killed, and so would the rest of our family. Even now that Ma is gone and our household stands at three, he was still never meant to exist. His life would cost us all of ours.

It's a raw deal, but he doesn't know the half of it. He's never had to risk his life to get food. He'll never understand why I come home out of breath, having run away from someone who caught me with a hand in their pocket. Fortunately, I'm quick. I know how to survive. But my precious Jonah will stay here for the rest of his life, waiting on me, and the only risk he will take is breathing when he shouldn't be here. That has to be enough.

His body seems to creak as he turns toward me. His whole body has suffered from his lifetime indoors. He might never be able to live a normal life. I worry if he tries to walk far, his legs might snap. But I guess he has nowhere to go anyway. I tell myself that it could be worse.

He's drawing on the wall of his alcove with charcoal. He doesn't have a lot of world experience, so he doesn't have much to draw. But he's good. I think that once, in a different life, maybe he could have gone to art school and learned to hone his skills, but we don't have use for that kind of thing in our country anymore. We're more preoccupied with feeding ourselves. Only the richest in society can stop to consider the beauty of things that are unaffordable to most. Families like the Goldings have gorgeous paintings on every inch of their walls, and books on shelves that reach the ceiling, and a turntable to play music. It's a fashion statement. But pretty colors on a canvas don't feed your family. Nor do books, a special privilege to have and to hold, especially when most people don't know how to read. Once, Ma's angelic voice was enough to give us a good life, but that's a talent that died with her.

Even if things changed now and Jonah had the chance to go to school, the cramps in his hands are too bad for him to work. Lately, he hasn't been able to hold his charcoal stick for longer than ten minutes before they hurt too much to continue. This poor child has been forsaken by this world before he's even been able to experience it.

"Where's Pa?" I ask, setting my bag on the table. I haven't reminded Jonah of what day it is, and I'm trying to seem jovial for his sake. Besides, I'm excited to see what Wren had packed for us, though I don't want to get Jonah's hopes up too much. Jonah smiles, continuing to draw on the wall.

"He went to the market."

I roll my eyes when Jonah's not looking. He doesn't mean the market I just visited. He means the black market, located in the basement of an apartment building three blocks over. I'm not entirely sure where it is – I have no desire to know. Pa's probably squandering his week's earnings on alcohol. And he wonders why we barely have enough food to line our stomachs. I'd work if I could, but I'm useless as far as this world if concerned. I don't have a trade. I used to do well at school, but it wasn't hard to pass the basic tests they set us. Maybe if I could have afforded to continue in education, I could have done better by my family.

Money's everything, really. If you've got it, you can afford to get the latest drugs. You can get TMS, some sort of magnetic pulse that improves your brain, and get so smart you end up with a scholarship to university. That way, you can get a job in medicine, or at least snatch up a job in Pink Light city, two of the most useful trades around. If you've got a little less money, you might be able to afford the pills that keep you up for hours and allow you to work for longer without sleeping, meaning you're an asset to any employer. Even a terrible job is better than no job. If I was offered the chance to do manual labor, or stamp ration cards day after day, I would. But I can't. If you haven't got money, this is what you get. I could get paid to take part in drug trials, but from what I've heard, those drugs are sometimes a fate worse than death. Even I'm not that desperate.

"Are you hungry, Jonah?" I ask him. A stupid question, but he nods enthusiastically. I fish in my pocket for the food Wren gave to me. It's tied up with a long piece of old ribbon. I remember the days when Wren used to wear those in her hair and I always envied her for it. Now, I slide the silky ribbon off the package and tie it around my wrist. It makes my heart flutter to own something so beautiful.

As I unwrap the brown wax paper, I find inside things that I've only dreamed of in recent years. Dried crispy bacon. A hunk of white bread. A sachet of pumpkin seeds. An orange. Damn, I haven't seen an orange in years. I bring it up to my nose to smell it. The citrusy aroma brings tears to my eyes. How long has Wren been saving to give me these things?

I wrap the food back up calmly. I have to make it last. But I can let Jonah indulge a little. I take the white crusty bread to him.

"Wipe your fingers, Jonah. I've got something for you."

He wipes the charcoal from his fingers and grins as he holds out his tiny palms. When I put the bread in his hands, his face lights up.

"For me?"

"For you."

Like me, he sniffs it, almost suspiciously. Then he gnaws at the bread eagerly. I smile and sit back to watch him enjoy it. My stomach is rumbling, but the sight of him enjoying himself makes me forget that for a moment. Maybe tonight I'll eat something from the care package. But for now, I'm content. It satisfies me more to see him happy.

I hear the door open. I turn and see Pa stagger through the door. I can tell from the misty look in his eyes he's been drinking. He doesn't look at either Jonah or I as he settles himself on his mattress, closing his eyes and blocking out the world as usual.

Jonah's face is hopeful as he crawls out of his alcove towards Pa. He shakes his arm and Pa opens his bloodshot eyes.

"Pa, did you see what I drew today?"

Pa sits up, but he doesn't look at Jonah's charcoal sketches. He takes a bottle from beneath his threadbare jacket and anger flares inside me. He promised not to bring alcohol home, back when he still had some respect left for me. Now, he's forgotten any promises he might have made. That tends to happen when you drown yourself in liquor.

I snatch the bottle from his hand. His body jerks, as though I just slapped him.

"Pa. How about you try and sober up and take a look at your son's drawing?"

He's not listening. He's just staring at the bottle clasped in my sweaty palms. I wonder what he might do to get it back. Would he strike me? He never has before, but the darkness inside him has been getting worse. His hand trembles as he raises it toward me. He's crossing the line between desperation and fury. I can feel my own hands beginning to shake. I don't want to know what comes next.

When I hear the high pitched wail on the speaker outside, Pa turns towards it, and I let myself breathe out. The siren is signaling a television broadcast.

It must be something important. Announcements are few and far between, and only ever made by government officials. I know from Wren that there are government reforms taking place to handle the overpopulation crisis. Maybe that's what this is about.

Since we don't have a TV, I shove the window open as wide as it will go and clamber onto the window sill next to the buckets we use to collect rainwater, my legs dangling over the streets. From here, I can see the corner of the huge screen that's suspended above the marketplace for these special broadcasts. Many people fill out into the square to hear better, but from here, I can already see the Prime Minister, Alastair Fairfax. His meaty chin hovers in the corner of the screen for a moment before he shifts out of my view.

Static echoes across the square from his microphone and Pa joins me on the window sill, his face blank. He smells so strongly of alcohol that I feel a little nauseous but I say nothing. Our feud can wait a while.

I glance at Jonah and see the curiosity in his eyes, but he has to stay in his alcove. We don't want him to be caught out, even if all attention appears to be on the screen. It's not worth the risk

"Good morning, Britain. I hope that you are all able to hear me today. We are in the wake of a new era today. The policies that have been discussed in parliament will affect each and every one of you...and big changes are coming for you all. In these tough times, we must learn to adapt. And that is what I am here to discuss today."

I almost sigh. Government plans never seem to do much. They always talk about a brighter future, and yet somehow the rich get richer and the poor stay in poverty. It seems to me that the likes of Alistair Fairfax are more interested in covering their own backs than saving the rest of us.

"Our country is in a mess of its own making," Fairfax continues. "We saw the signs and never stopped them. We didn't control our immigration. We didn't restrict family sizes soon enough. We didn't learn to be self-sufficient until it was too late. Ceasing our trading within the European Union left us with few options, and there was no going back. We were left with barren land from wars. But we found ways to produce food. We've managed to survive in a difficult political, social and environmental climate. We formed new political parties to handle each crisis as it came our way. We are, as many will agree, a success story."

I roll my eyes to myself. Not one person I know would believe that. Historically, politicians like to tell us they're succeeding while basking in their own failures.

"We have come to a decision today as a government that we believe will be beneficial to our people. This is a time in which difficult decisions must be made, to ensure our survival as a race. We've watched the rest of the world cut down more and more of their populations, in ways that we have always deemed inhumane. And now, it's time to consider whether they were right."

My chest tightens as the Prime Minister clears his throat, shifting again. I know what he's referring to. The things we all prefer not to talk about to pretend they didn't happen outside of our country. The mass extermination camps. The poisoned water sources abroad to kill the poor. We turned a blind eye to it all because at least it wasn't us. At least we got to live.

But our country is just as bad; fighting pits to entertain the rich and slay the poor souls who can't afford to feed themselves without killing others for sport. Extortionate health care prices to ensure that those in poor areas don't live past their teens, following the decimation of our country's free health service. The reintroduction of the death penalty in all countries, doled out for petty crimes. I could've been hanged a hundred times over for stealing by now. The world is already cruel. What can the government possibly have in mind to make things worse?

"We have been in self-destruct mode for hundreds of years. We've watched our planet slowly being destroyed by our actions. Our greed is killing us."

Our greed or yours? I think bitterly, but Fairfax continues regardless. "We never did heed the warnings we were given. Now, we live on a planet where trees are a rare sight. Where the number of people outnumbers the amount of food we can produce. Where we have to fight and scrounge just to get scraps."

"Some more than others," I mutter. Pa's lips twitch into an almost smile, but I'm too anxious to share the rare moment where we're getting along.

"We need to change. We've evolved over the years, but we are not fit for this world we've created. We need to speed up the process. We need to become better. Stronger. Smarter." He pauses. Everyone in the square is holding their breath.

"We must adapt to survive. Our new programme will ensure we do."

I can't help thinking back to the government's last 'programme' – the strain of flu they released into the air, killing off hundreds of thousands of people. It was the biggest epidemic in the history of our country. It led to the Prime Minister, Agatha Redknapp, being hanged outside parliament by mobs of protesters: they made the noose out of her tie. It broadcast live and there were parties in the streets.

"We have been researching a drug that will make us better – allow us to reach our full potential. The X drug enhances the most ordinary of us. It can make normal folk physically strong, mentally enhanced and practically invincible. At a price, this drug can help you reach your optimum. But if these drugs are to be beneficial, if we are to be better as a whole, and not just as individuals, we must first...cut back."

And there it is.

"We must reduce our numbers further. Everyone must take a survey to see if they are applicable for the new drugs. Our next generation must be built on the smartest, strongest people alive so that our future may be secure in their hands."

"And what about the rest of us?" Pa mutters. I can smell the liquor on his breath. "What about us..."

"Those who are not deemed eligible or cannot afford the fees for the pills will no longer have access to ration cards. Those who make themselves self-sufficient will be allowed to continue living in their residences and paving the way to our new future. But we must ask that each of you considers what you might offer. Think about the future of humanity. Think about what sacrifices you can make to ensure the survival of life itself."

I can hear people beginning to scream and shout in the streets. They're beginning to understand the fact that is just sinking in for me too. That we're disposable to them. That they want us gone so that they can begin some new life with the best of the best.

And we aren't among them.

"We are offering free euthanasia to the first one hundred thousand citizens who willingly offer to give their lives so others may live-"

Alistair Fairfax's voice is drowned out by the commotion in the street, but it doesn't matter. I've heard enough. I swing my legs back into the flat, my face heating up as I slip back inside. We have to go. We have to get out of here before things get messy. People will riot over this. Everyone I know carries a weapon of some description. Blood will be spilled on all sides, and I don't intend to get involved. I think about the care package that Wren gave me. If ration cards will be revoked, who knows what someone might do to me in order to get their hands on that kind of food?

"Jonah, we're leaving."

"Where to?"

"I don't know, Jonah. We'll go somewhere else. Get to Pink Light City. Or make a boat, sail across the sea."

"You don't know how to do that. Raven-"

"Well, I guess I'll just have to learn then," I say, my mind whirring. I know I'm not talking sense, but I can feel desperation setting in already. "We can adapt. That's what they want, right? For us to adapt? They want us to show we can survive. So we've got to be smart about this. Get away from here, it's not safe. Isn't that right, Pa?"

Pa is still sitting on the window sill, the Prime Minister's words flooding around his ears. I take a tentative step towards him, but he shifts position on the ledge, and I stop, déjà vu rushing over me. I've been here before. Pa looks at me over his shoulder. I watch him swallow, a lump bobbing in his throat. His hands grip the window ledge. There's pain in his eyes that I recognize all too well.

"Pa…"

"I can't do this," he says simply. Then he pushes himself away and disappears over the ledge.

I don't run to try and catch him. I've played this scenario before, and I know how it ends. I just close my eyes and try not to hear the cries as his body hits the ground.

RILEY

I'm not known for having nice teeth, but if I don't move now, I'm not going to have any left at all. This girl is trying to jab her fist right into my gob. Usually, the Pits don't offer much competition, but today, I've got a hard opponent. Well, I say hard. I just have to make some effort, is all.

She throws another punch. I duck. Near miss. I roll my eyes, shuffling back. This gal reckons she's hard. She's circling me, teeth bared. She thinks she's scary, with her shaved head and a big-ass scar down her face. But that scar says that someone got her good. She wasn't quick enough. Which means she's stupid. Or slow.

Probably both.

I crack my neck, looking up at the stands. It's damn quiet today. Not many people can afford to bet at the minute, not even rich kids from uptown. But the sensible ones here are betting I'll win. They'll all go home with coins jangling in their pockets and tonight, I'll eat like a bloody queen. So long as I put on a good show. Which means toying with this girl before I finish her.

It's sweet that she thinks she's got a chance. Aren't many idiots around here willing to fight me. She bets 'cause she's stronger, 'cause she's older, she's gonna win. But guess what?

I'm smarter. And I've never lost a fight yet. If I had, I'd be dead, after all.

She's been holding back. She's only thrown a few punches. She's not even reached for her knife yet, and mine is still safely tucked on my belt. But she wants to. And when she does, I'll get her. But I've got to get my move just right. If not, it's bye bye Riley.

We're ten meters apart. I've been backing away steadily, ready for my move. She runs at me, but still I wait. Wait. Wait for it. Five meters. I set off at a run. I've got my eyes trained on where I'll hit – right in the stomach.

The shock on her face as I slam into her is priceless. My head butts hard into her stomach and I tackle her waist. I laugh as we tumble to the ground. Sometimes, this job is far too easy.

My hand slips onto her belt and takes her knife. As she lies on the floor, I hop back onto my feet. The crowd is cheering and I egg them on. All part of the fun. In their eyes, at least.

The girl is sweating as she stumbles to her feet. I twirl a knife in each of my hands. She knows she won't win now. She knows she'll die. For whatever reason, it doesn't stop her from running. Drawing it out. This is the chase the audience loves. I run after her, knives ready. She's breathless, sobbing. She keeps looking over her shoulder at me. Begging. But if our positions were swapped, she wouldn't show me mercy. If it's a choice between you and someone you don't know, you always know who you'll prioritize.

I feel bad, though. I'm too damn sympathetic for this line of work. I decide to throw her a lifeline. If I throw a knife and miss, she'll be able to claim it. I raise my arm.

Unfortunately for her, I never miss.

She's floored by her own knife. It whizzes through the air and lodges in her leg. She crashes to the ground. I skid to a halt by her fallen body. She's whimpering. This is the worst part. Because I can't kill her yet. The audience won't like that. If the audience isn't satisfied, I get nothing. And so I remove the knife from her leg and straddle her. She fights against me, but I pin down her wrist with her knife. She yowls and I close my eyes.

"You shouldn't have come here," I tell her. Then my knife gets to work as the crowd goes wild.

It takes me a bloody long time to wash the blood off. It's rooted in the lines in my palm. Dug under my nails. It stains up to my wrists, like gloves. The water turns red, then pink as it all washes down the drain. I like every spot to be gone. It's better that way.

Clean clothes. The smell of dinner cooking. The squeak of my shoes on clean floors. It's still unreal to me, sometimes. The place I used to call home was a tarpaulin that I shared with five girls and a mangy cat. Now, I have a hot shower every night and a bed to sleep in. I have food and clean water and clothes that aren't torn to shreds.

At the price of being a ring-fighter, of course.

I wonder who else survived their fights today. There were twelve fights, so twelve winners overall.

And twelve dead bodies.

The winners should already be here for dinner. That is, if none of them got beat up real bad. I'm sure the usual suspects will be joining me. I could bet on their fights if I had money, but I wouldn't anyway. I already gamble on my life every week. I don't want to do the same for the only people I can call friends.

When I stroll in the food hall, Squid stands up from our table, grinning at me, his gangly arms reaching out for me. "Phoenix, you little devil! Another win?"

I smile. I've always liked the nickname that Squid gave me when I arrived here. We all have one, but mine is the best. I rose from the ashes to become the fighter I am today. My flame-red hair might have had something to do with it too, but I like the metaphor better.

"You know it," I grin, leaping into his arms. He whirls me around in a circle then plops me on the floor and ruffles my hair.

"You did good, lil tyke," he says. There's a nick across his eyebrow today where a knife has sliced it open, but he's still smiling. "Come get some dinner."

I sit at the table beside him. The usual crew are here, the people I call my friends in this lawless place. Tiger, with his bulky frame and cautious pale eyes. Bull, the strongest and scariest of us all despite her short stature. Eagle, lithe and tall with hands like claws. But there's one spot missing at the table. I frown.

"Where's Pup?"

Squid and Tiger exchange a look. Tiger looks down at the table. I slap Squid's arm urgently.

"Tell me!"

"She got beat up real bad," Squid says, scratching at the stubble on the side of his head. "But they think she'll be okay. Try not to worry."

I do worry. Pup and I go way back. Way before the fighting pits. We were both orphans, both left to fend for ourselves out on the streets. We're the kids the world forgot about. We never went to school because our parents couldn't afford for us to go, and we never got registered for ration cards or IDs. The kids in downtown think they have it rough? Nuh-uh. Try having to steal everything you eat. Imagine how cold you get when it rains and the plastic over your head can't stop it soaking you. That's where me and Elianna – Pup – used to be.

But she was never made to be here. She's not a fighter. She wins her fights on luck, following her instincts and striking out at the last moment to save her skin. The audience loves an underdog, I suppose, and it earned her her nickname. She's managed to walk away mostly unscathed so far, but I guess her luck has finally run out. I slump in my seat.

"Damn. What do I do?"

"Nothing you can do," Bull says, propping her heavy boots on the table. There's blood matted in her short dark hair. "Dinner's coming soon, anyway."

"How can you think about food now?" Tiger says. He's twitching, his freckled face paler than normal. He doesn't look like much – this skinny, tall boy with hair the color of carrots. Everyone says he doesn't live up to his name. But they ain't seen him fight. When he fights, there's a new man out there. A man who can tear you to shreds. He's got the same advantage that Pup and I have – we're stronger than we seem.

"Relax, Tiger. Injuries are in the job description," Eagle says, rolling her beady eyes. "Like Bull says. Ain't nothing we can do. We earned this meal. So we're going to enjoy it. Don't have a face on, or you can eat outside."

They've got a point. Tiger looks at me for support, but I shrug. People die in the Pits. It happens. That's the point. But they have good doctors here. All we can do is pray they do a good job with Elianna.

Servers bring out platters of food that take up every inch of space on the table. I stab my fork in cuts of beef, pork, chicken. I scoop vegetables onto my plate until they're piled high. Potatoes follow. Thick gravy. Tiger stays stubborn for a few minutes as we eat. Then he starts to pile food onto his own plate. After all, this is what we fight for. We fight, we eat, we fight, we eat. And no matter how dark that seems, it still feels good to line our stomachs, especially when we know how it feels to starve.

"So good," I mumble through a mouthful of food. Table manners don't matter. Not when you dine with street rats.

"Enjoy this while you can, Phoenix. That was your last fight."

I turn mid mouthful. It's the boss – Lion. She watches us with watery eyes, her lips pursed. Her black suit has shoulder pads that look like mini wings. I screw up my face.

"What the hell are you talking about?"

"The Pits are closing, girl. Didn't any of you hear the announcement?"

"What announcement?"

She shakes her head. "Of course. You were all in the Pit during. New government scheme. They're creating some kind of super-human race. They inject you with something that makes you super smart and super strong. They're calling it the X drug. If you've got three grand spare, feel free to sign up for it. They'd like you. You've got the strength they're looking for, and the brains."

Of course I don't have three grand. Who does? No one I know. I shake my head. "So what? What's that got to do with our fights?"

"You think anyone's going to pay for bets on the pits when they could be spending it on the X drug?"

"Err, yes? There will be plenty of people who don't have the dosh for the X drug. If they make smart bets, they'll have cash in their pocket in no time."

"Riley, you don't get it. They're not just making super-humans. They're killing everyone else off. There will be no more system, no ration cards, no help from the government. It'll be every man for themselves, and the rich will be doing just fine so long as they can pay for the drugs. You see now? They'll come after you kids anytime now. I can't support you here any more."

"Fuck that," Squid says, standing up. "You've been good to us. As good as any money grabbing asshole can be. But you can't just stop now. You can't let us just die."

"I don't have a business anymore. It's going to crash and burn. I'd rather get out with my money while I can. I can get the X drug. I filled out my survey already – I'm sure I'll be eligible," Lion says, placing her hands behind her back. Squid squares up to her, the veins on his neck pulsing.

"You said you'd look after us. It's a two-way street. We provide your entertainment, and you feed us. That's how it works."

Lion pushes Squid back. The force surprises him so much he falls back. Normally I'd revel in the drama, but I leap to Squid's side to steady him. Lion's eyes are narrowed.

"I don't owe you anything. If I finish my business, then

the deal ends. That's how it is."

Lion starts to walk away and I stand to grab her arm. "Wait one second. Are you telling us you don't care at all about what happens to us?"

Lion squirms. "Of course I do." She straightens her jacket. "But I have to think of myself."

"Then do one last thing for us. A special fight, that will bring lots of people in to bet."

The room is silent for a moment. I might have found us a lifeline. Lion raises an eyebrow. "Go on."

I look back at the others. They nod at me in encouragement. I'm going to have to improvise. "Something the audience can't resist. You could advertise it as your two best fighters going into the pit together. The outcome would be unpredictable. Exciting. You could take half of the earnings, and we could split the rest between us. It'll keep us going for a while, at least. Everyone's a winner."

"Except whoever winds up dead," Eagle scoffs. "You think any of us are dumb enough to sign up for this, Phoenix? You're talking about one of us killing another of us."

The thought makes me wanna spew. But I play it cool, shrugging. "If we don't, we'll wind up dead. We'll starve out on the street, or get hunted down. Would you rather die like that, or die fighting?"

That shuts her up. But Tiger's shaking his head. "How are we meant to choose who goes in the Pits, then? There's no way in hell I would volunteer for that. Not when I'd be fighting my friends."

Everyone's looking to me for an answer. I roll my eyes. "It's obvious. The good old fashioned name out of a hat. All five of us."

"What about Pup?" Bull says dumbly.

"Sure. Why not? She could have one arm for all we know, but yeah, let's get her back in the Pits. Of course not her, dumbass."

Squid sniggers and Bull purses her lips, folding her arms.

"Fine. Let's just get on with it, shall we?"

Lion produces a notepad from her jacket and writes each of our names on a scrap of paper. Everyone's eyeing each other up. One of us has to kill one of us. That's a damn scary thought. I stand close to Squid. He ruffles my hair, but his eyes are fixed on the pieces of paper. Lion folds them up and grabs an empty bowl for us to pick out of.

"Well? Who wants to do it?" Eagle snaps. Her legs are shaking. Tiger steps forwards.

"I will," he says quietly. I hold my breath as his hand delves into the bowl. His hand trembles as he unfolds the paper.

"Harper."

It takes me a second to remember that's Eagle's real name. Her face turns very pale and she nods silently. Tiger's hand jumps straight back in the hat and my heart lodges in my throat. *Not me. Not me.* Tiger opens the paper. Squid reaches for my hand and squeezes it. I can't breathe.

Tiger swallows. He looks up. His eyes meet Bull's. She gasps, tears stinging her eyes. She looks at Eagle, reaching out for a hug. Eagle slaps her hand away and storms out of the room, slamming the door behind her. But it's not me. It's selfish to think, but thank God it wasn't me. Thank God it wasn't Squid. Now that I think about it, it's the best possible turnout. Squid and Tiger matter more to me, and all of us are safe. All of us will walk away from the Pits with more money than we've ever had before.

We'll just walk away with one less friend.

KARISSA

The hard metal bench I rest on to undo my boots makes my bruises seem even sorer. It was combat training this morning, and Captain Strauss put me up against Biff from Team Seven. Like I stood a chance. We have a completely different skill set, and I was set up to lose from the start. But I fought hard and long and didn't stop until I passed out, like I've always been taught. I want to prove I have what it takes to be a soldier. I want to earn my place.

But it looks bad for me, and now, back in our dorm, the others snigger at me. They, of course, saw the whole thing, and there's no hiding the fact that I was beaten when Biff has left his mark all over my body. Elliott whispers to Minerva and she smirks, staring at me. I stare back until she squirms away. It's the only defense I have left.

I'm not weak, just because I'm weaker. My body is smaller, sleeker; I'm made to dodge punches, not to throw them. My arms are strong, stronger than most, but not stronger than the strongest man I know. It's science. How can I be stronger and bigger when I am built for smaller things?

My mind is as sharp as any. I've passed every test they've thrown at me. I'm smart, quick witted, able. I can run faster than most of the soldiers at the Institute, and I'm light on my feet, making me stealthy. I am an excellent shot, I have a high pain threshold, and I keep the others on their toes. I have all the makings of a great soldier, and in theory, I should be well-liked and respected for that.

So why don't they like me?

I just have to ignore them. We're not allowed to have feelings in this line of work. Too costly. And yet I can't stop watching Minnie. We've trained together since the age of eight, but it's like I'm only just noticing her now, suddenly feeling the need for her approval. I've heard people talk about crushes before, but I think this is my first. I see her and I feel something strange stirring in my stomach. Something like adrenaline, something like the kick of the X drug, but more subdued, more constant. My heart crashes against my chest, the way it does when we do parachute training, but this feeling is more welcome.

I'm not the only one looking. She's used to making sure people are always looking. She openly coaxes Elliott with her flirtatious jokes, loving his eyes roaming over her body. She teases Zach, who watches her hungrily, but I know she'll let him starve before she gives herself to him. She ignores Ronan almost completely, but he watches her all the same in his quiet, desperate way. She's got the whole team looking at her.

She stands out from the rest of us. When we were kids, she figured out how to make her lips a different color. She stole red food coloring from the kitchen, and mixed it with our prescribed aloe vera lip balm. Now, her lips are always red, like she's been eating too many strawberries.

But it looks good. So does her hair swept high, waves of blonde arching up and then dipping down past her shoulders. She's done up the top button of her jumpsuit. Some girls have copied her, but not to the same effect. Her jumpsuit is tight on her, snug on the curves of her body. Deliberately. She's technically not breaking the dress code, but I can tell Captain Strauss doesn't like the way she presents herself.

We're soldiers, not models, she often points out. And I agree with her. But it doesn't mean I don't like to look.

There's something admirable about the way she acts. It's her own personal rebellion, I think. She didn't ask to be here, like the rest of us. Apart from Elliott, that is. But this is the life we're destined to live until the day we die, so I guess sooner or later, she'll have to come around to that fact and follow the rules. After all, we're soldiers, and that's what we're supposed to do. It's not a surprise to any of us. None of us have left this place in eight years, since our tenth birthdays. We knew even then that the next time we left here would be to go to war on the common folk. Now, we're just waiting for that time to come.

Then our lives will truly begin.

I should relax. It's pain endurance class later today. I need to be ready. This time is designated for getting some sleep and replenishing. But I can still hear the others chatting, laughing at something Zach said. Him and Ronan aren't so bad; Zach's the clown of the team, and Ronan's quiet, smart, keeps to himself mostly. Marcia's okay too. A little on the dopey side, and slower than the others. Yet she fits in better than I do.

If it wasn't for Elliott, I'd be okay.

He's got it in for me. Because he was the one who trained so hard to get in. After I was selected at the age of six to train at the Institute part time from all the students at our school, it became his goal to get into the programme too. He was the only one who ever volunteered. Our lives were at risk when they tried out various drugs on us. Our bodies were bone tired, forced to their limits every day. But because I was doing it, he had to too. That was how he always was. Desperate to compete. Desperate to win.

He had a later start than I did. As a child, his bones were riddled with rickets and allergies prevented him doing a lot of things he longed to. While he was treated, he was in a wheelchair, wired up to respiratory support. It cost our parents everything they had to keep him alive. That was until

I came here, and I began to send money to them each week from the researchers here at the Institute. That was when he became reliant on me.

I used to be allowed to go home every weekend, and whenever I saw Elliott, he was quiet and thoughtful, glaring at me all the time. Every time I left to come back to the Institute, he'd watch with jealous fire in his eyes. One time, when I was younger, I came home with a badge pinned to my chest. It read 'Top of the Class' in red bubble writing. That day I'd been the first in the hundred-meter race, completing it in 13.45 seconds. It seemed impressive at the time, and my parents were so proud. But later, after Mum turned out the lights in our room, I heard Elliott crying in the dark. And I wish I'd gone to him then, but I didn't.

Something must have changed that day, because Elliott started getting better, almost as though through sheer determination. And when he was well enough to train like all the other kids our age, he threw himself into it, like a lion on a piece of meat. He used to get up early before school and run for an hour, then swim for an hour, then practise weights. All before eight o'clock. Then he'd go to class smelling of chlorine and sweat, and study until lunch, at which point he'd grab a snack and go running again. Rain or shine, he'd be out on that school field, curls plastered to his face. Other kids would laugh at him, wearing his protective mask to help him breathe. They'd say he looked stupid. They accused him of smelling bad in class, when he'd sit there with his armpits and back drenched in sweat. But he didn't care one bit. Getting on the programme was all that mattered to him.

And Elliott is smart. So much smarter than my parents, than me, the researchers here. Smart in a way that can't be taught; witty, sarcastic, manipulative. He's good with strategy, calculations, and he understands science. He has a way with words, a certain charm, a tongue like a knife. What he lacks in speed and stamina, he makes up for in smarts. And then just before our tenth birthday, he turned up at the Institute, ready to take part in the next round of Trials.

It's felt like we've been neck and neck ever since. I never saw much sport in competing with him. I'm not interested in beating him. But he's always made our lives a contest. He puts so much effort into everything he does.

But I always feel a sense of ease in the challenges put before us. I might not be the strongest here, which can be a disadvantage, but the rest of the tasks that we're assigned feel easy enough to me. I relax into them. Let my body do the thinking. I love the burn in my muscles as I run, the raw feeling in my throat when I'm out of breath, the feel of fresh bruises blossoming on my arms during hand to hand combat. We're given puzzles to do in the evening. Riddles, advanced reading, equations. Where my other classmates see chore, I see leisure, but also challenge. Something to sink my teeth into. Elliott loves it too. It's his obsession. For years, he barely spoke to anyone, all his time and efforts spent on training. But now, he's the one with friends. The one everyone likes. He's smooth that way. The better version of me, even after everything he went through to get here.

I ignore Minnie's giggles as I get into my bunk and try to sleep, knowing that Elliott is the reason no one will give me the time of day.

And that's the reason that I resent him.

We're used to pain and taking a hit here, but it's not often we're woken with a punch to the stomach. I lurch upwards, gasping out, but my fists are already balled up, ready. I blink through the sleep in my eyes, seeing my brother looming over me. He grins.

"Fancy some extra combat training?" he asks sweetly.

I'm on my feet in an instant, slipping my feet into my boots and tying them as fast as I can. It takes me a moment to realize that the others have formed a sort of circle around our dormitory. Like a fighting ring. Is that what this is?

"Don't you ever sleep?" I ask wearily.

Elliott ignores me. "What do you say, sis? You up for a

fight? Or are you chicken?" I fold my arms tiredly, bored of his stupid game. To my surprise, it makes Minnie smirk. Elliott is glaring at me.

"Come on, Karissa," he murmurs, raising an eyebrow. "Show me what you've got. I thought you wanted to be the best?"

The others look at me expectantly. I do. I do want to be the best. I want to give these people a reason to care that I exist for once. I draw my shoulders back as I step forwards in acceptance. I have nothing to lose here. And despite Elliott's improvements, this is a fight I should probably win. I've always avoided fighting him in combat classes, mostly because I feel I owe him something; for the head start I had in life. I don't want to ruin his credibility, show him up. But for once, I'm glad I'm facing him. I'm tired of his attitude. I'm sick of him trying to subdue me, push me down, make me feel unwanted. We stare at each other, sizing one another up, searching for weaknesses. I'm going to beat you down.

"This will be fun," Elliott says quietly in amusement. But I'm ready for the punch he throws a second later. A predictable move. His eyes gave away exactly what he was going to do. I make out like I'm about to copy his motion and he grabs my wrist, but he isn't expecting the knee to his groin maneuver that doubles him over. I have the upper hand. Still reluctant to hurt him much, I allow him a second to get back to his feet. It's foolish of me. I narrowly dodge an elbow thrust to my abdomen and hurtle back to my bunk to get away. I have no time to compose myself as Elliott runs at me. So I run too. I'm small enough that I can dodge around him, making towards the bunk that Minnie and Marcia share. I need some time to prepare myself. I leap up onto the ladder on Minnie's bed, and, as Elliott sprints towards me, I swing my legs from the ladder, watching my feet slam into Elliott's chest. He falls to the floor, and I hear Minnie cackle. That gives me a new surge of energy. I jump down from the ladder and stand over him, ready to kick his smug face, but he grabs my ankle and I flail for a moment before crashing to the ground next to him, a shoot of pain rushing through my spine. I let my ego get the better of me, but it won't happen again.

Elliott grins as he and I wrestle. He seems to think we were bonding or something. Like two children just playing. But we're not. I struggle with him, finally gaining dominance when I pin his arms to his side with my knees. He struggles beneath me, but my hold on him is strong. I glare down at him, but he merely smiles, and I see the boy he was when we were young. Carefree, smiling, loving. Weak.

He's changed so much.

"Finish it," he says, "Go on. Smash my face in. You know you want to."

"Do you really want me to?" I ask. I'm trying to sound threatening, but I want to hear his answer.

"They want you to," he hisses. I look over at my teammates. They're watching in awe, waiting for me to make a move. They want an ending to this fight. They want to know what I'm capable of. I raise my fist, ready to slam it into his face.

"Soldier Gray?"

I know that voice. I follow it to the dormitory door. Captain Strauss is staring at me. I quickly stand and salute.

"Captain."

She looks down at Elliott on the floor, then back to me, looking slightly disturbed. *Isn't this what you want, Captain? Someone willing to fight?*

"Come with me," she says quietly. I look back at my teammates. They're all staring at me. I make to follow Captain Strauss, but Elliott stands and grabs my arm just before I can.

"You missed your chance," he whispered. "Next time, I'll win. And I won't hesitate to crush you. We should be ruthless, Karissa. We're battle born, after all."

"You don't have to keep doing this," I say softly. "We don't have to be at one another's throats. We used to be…we used to be friends."

Elliott grins at me. "How sweet. You thought we were friends? You thought you mattered to me?" He leans in closer, his eyes full of a miserable kind of anger. "All I have ever wanted is to show everyone how they favored the wrong twin. Nothing else. And I'll prove it yet."

I'm getting sick of this. There's no changing his mind. I shake him off. "Did this teach you nothing?" I lean close to his ear, my face burning. "You can't beat me. You'll never...*ever*, be good enough."

Elliott's face contorts in shock, but I'm not sticking around to watch him crumble. I've given him a thousand chances, but this was the last straw. Captain Strauss is waiting for me, and whatever she needs from me matters more than my brother's hurt feelings.

I don't know what she could possibly want, though. I wonder if I'm being punished for my tussle with Elliott. Not likely. It's something she'd usually encourage, since it builds up our skills. So why the fuss, during rest time?

Her office is the only part of the building with a good view. The large open window overlooks our training grounds. Team Seven have just returned from last night's expedition, and they're gathered out in the courtyard. Like all the teams, they're in the process of picking Team Captains and Seconds, but to me, it seems Team Seven already has their leader. I know her. Her name is Adelaide. She's got the highest IQ score in the whole of the twelve teams under Captain Strauss' command. She's small and slight, like me, but fast and strong.

"What do you see?" Captain Strauss asks me. I watch Adelaide out the window, wondering what the Captain wants me to say.

"A Team Captain," I say after a while.

"And what does a Team Captain do?"

"They captain?" I say wearily. I'm not in the mood for her guessing games. I try not to wince as she clips me around the back of the head.

"Don't make me change my mind about you. I want you to tell me the qualities of a good Team Captain."

I watch as Adelaide begins to march her team back inside, and analyze her. "Strength. Team building. Charisma. Skill."

"Good. What else?"

"Bravery. Honesty. Ruthlessness." I pause and think of my brother, primed for the position as Team Captain. He has the one thing I don't. " But…they need to be loved too."

"They need to be respected, not loved," Captain Strauss argues. She sits down at her desk, her beady black eyes watching me. "Do you think I'm well loved, Karissa? Do you think my job makes people affectionate towards me?"

I don't know how to respond. No one likes Captain Strauss. She's all the things I mentioned and more. She can be cruel, bossy, and hateful. But there's one thing she certainly is.

"Respected." I try out the word on my lips. Captain Strauss nods, almost sadly.

"It can come at a cost. But sometimes, respect is the one thing you're missing that could make you a good leader." She leans forwards, her arms folded on her desk "What you lack, Soldier, is respect. Your brother has held you back for some time, and I believe that if that were to change, you would make the perfect leader for your team."

"You…you do?"

"Absolutely. In fact, I'd encourage it. You have something that your brother lacks completely. You have raw talent. He's smart, and so are you, but he will never match your physical skills. And when you build on that talent, the results are so much better than those who work hard, but never had that special something to start with. It's sad, but it's true. I was like your brother. And it's not to say that he will be unsuccessful. But I have faith in you. I think as Team Captain, you could build a winning team. You could easily make your team one of the best by the time it comes for you to go to battle. Which, I can assure you, will be very soon."

"But that doesn't matter. Like you said. I'm not respected. Not the way Elliott is. I'd never get elected as Team Captain."

Captain Strausss studies me in interest. "You think Elliott

would win the vote?"

"Or Minnie. Either could do it. Minnie has the charisma and team-building skills. Elliott has the ruthlessness. People admire him for that."

"But the combination of the two is the ideal."

"What are you saying?"

Captain Strauss smiles; a rare sight. "I'm saying that you need to prepare, Karissa. Over the next week, there are going to be changes. Tonight, you proved to the rest of your team that you have something admirable, something they can rally behind. Go back to your dorm and rest now. This afternoon's training is postponed. But keep up the good work. Keep your team interested. And wait."

For what? I want to ask. But I've learnt its best not to question Captain Strauss. If she wants to say something, she'll say it. I take it as my cue to leave, and shut the door behind me on my way out.

Back in the dormitory, all is quiet. The lights have been turned out for rest time. But there's someone sitting on my bunk. Minnie's legs are crossed, her hands behind her as she leans against them. She's smiling that red lipped smile. Chest stuck out. Eyebrow arched. I almost stumble.

She's trying to impress me.

"Hey," she purrs. "That was a cool stunt you pulled."

I pause in front of my bed, looking down at her.

"Stunt?"

She smirks. "Taking Elliott down like that. I never knew you had it in you. I guess I was wrong about you."

"And what impression did you have previously?"

Minnie leans forwards, elbow on her knee. "I thought you were weak. But you've got something…good. You're strong." Her lips pout a little. I think she might be flirting with me. I'm not used to it. My stomach twists into a knot. Isn't this what I've been hoping for all along.

"Maybe I shouldn't be wasting my time on your brother," she whispers, looking up at me from under dark eyelashes. I swallow down a lump in my throat. I want her to want me, I really do. But not like this. Not after everything I've been put through. *If you have any self-reverence, you won't let her worm her way in so fast.*

"You're on my bed. In my way," I say flatly. Minnie blinks, her mask slipping for a moment and revealing her shock. I raise my eyebrow.

"But…"

"Beat it," I tell her. She hesitates for a second. She doesn't like being told what to do. I hear sniggering from one of the bunks. Zach and Ronan are laughing at her.

"Shut up," Minnie hisses into the dark as she stands up and flounces back to her own bunk. She looks back at me, her face bearing something that looks like offense. I slide into bed without a backwards glance, facing the wall so no one can see my smile.

Maybe part of the key to others respecting you is respecting yourself.

RAVEN

Jonah's in shock. Who can blame him when his entire world has just fallen apart? I've tried feeding him some of the soup I made, but he refuses to part his lips. He's just staring ahead of him, eyes glazed over. I try to eat some soup myself, but for once, I'm not hungry. I abandon it and pull Jonah close to me, tugging a blanket over our knees. I try not to let my fear become physical, but still I tremble.

Some time passes. I don't know how much. Jonah falls asleep against my shoulder. Out in the streets, I can hear the commotion. Probably people protesting. People like me – people who can't afford a loaf of bread most weeks, let alone fancy drugs. People like me, who will lose everything, including our lives. People like me who aren't ready to die, but aren't being given a choice.

I wonder how they will try to cull us. They tried it once, and now, they've learned from their mistakes. A flu virus is too unreliable, not targeted enough. Perhaps they have a hidden army ready to strike against us. Perhaps they'll round us up and throw us all in a fighting pit for entertainment. Maybe they will put daggers in the hands of the rich and let them hunt us for sport. It won't be long before the rich realize that their immunity will grant them the ability to do whatever they want. Then, cruel hearts will set themselves on the likes of us.

I know there's somewhere Jonah and I can go. Logan told me he'd take care of us if ever we needed it. But I can't go begging to him. Not now. I've not seen him since Ma killed herself. It wasn't his fault, but it was his father's, at least partially. I can't go to him for charity, not even to save myself. Not even to save Jonah.

No. I'm going to have to figure something out myself. It's a big world out there, and we've only seen what's in a ten-mile radius of us. I've never made it further. I've seen maps of our country from years ago. Britain used to be a land of green and farmland. Now, there's barely an inch of land left untouched. Some people try to be self-sufficient by growing their own vegetables, especially outside of the cities where it's more rural, but it's almost impossible in the high rises. We don't get enough sun outside our windows to grow much, and all rainwater is polluted. We have to boil it up to make it suitable to drink.

Everything we grow in this country is in Pink Light City. I've only ever seen pictures, but it's beautiful – a city of glass skyscrapers, all filled with plants in various stages of bloom. It's a place that can literally be viewed through rose-tinted glass. It's where you work if you're lucky, and it's where I always dreamed of working. I always wanted to spend my day with tomato vines and apple trees towering over my head, the smell of oranges and pears filling my nose. But to get there, you need a decent education or some knowledge of agriculture, which I don't have.

Maybe now, I can find Pink Light City. Maybe by some stroke of luck I'll find a job there to support me and Jonah. The land of plenty. It's a pipedream, I know. I could turn left outside our building and go in the complete wrong direction. I might never find it, and even if I do, they will likely turn me away. But it's a start. It's a goal to aim for. Where else can I hope to go?

I shift Jonah off my shoulder and jump to my feet. I need

to pack for us. It only takes me a moment to realize it won't take long. Our two cupboards are bare aside from our loaf of bread, several gnarled carrots and Wren's care package. The soup I made earlier is sitting cold on the counter – I'll pack it up and take it in our flask. Then there's only our tin bowls and spoons, one sharp knife and our blankets. I sold all of Ma's clothes that she was gifted by Alec Golding years ago, but that money is gone now. Everything else we own we wear on our backs.

And all of a sudden, I'm glad Pa's dead. If he were here now, I'd want to kill him. His selfishness has left us with nothing. He drank all our money away, oblivious to our suffering because of it. Now, we don't own a thing. He didn't care about us. Maybe he did once. But since Ma died, he's been lost to us. I clench my fists, trying to stay calm, and remind myself we're better off without him. The pain of his loss stabs at me, but the anger I feel is like a comforting blanket somehow.

I'm going to make sure we're okay now. I'm going to be better to this family than he ever was. Starting with the decision to leave this place for good.

I wrap all our supplies up in my blanket and fashion it into a sack I can sling over my back. I leave the knife out, tucking it onto my belt. Then I shake Jonah gently. He turns over, his body practically creaking with the effort. I try for a smile.

"We have to go now, Jonah. We're not staying here."

"I can't go outside," Jonah protests. "Someone will see me."

"Things have changed. That's not our concern anymore. We're all in danger, do you understand? Everyone without a job or skill or money is worthless, and we have none of those things. We have no choice. We have to go. Come on."

"Don't we want to make a plan?"

"We'll plan as we go...if anyone asks, you're my son, okay?" It might work. He looks younger than seven and I look older than seventeen. If no one thinks we're siblings, we can hope that no one flags us up. We don't need any more reasons to be stopped in the street.

"Time to go. Now, Jonah."

Jonah's eyes widen, but he nods, hoisting himself to his knees. It's only as he struggles to stand that I notice how bad his legs have become. Below his knees, his legs jut out at odd angles, like snapped matchsticks. He winces as he tries to move, and I know right off he won't be able to walk far. But he tries anyway, taking my hand and waddling to the door. I take one last look at our small, rotting home; the bare wooden walls, Jonah's alcove, our black crusted stove. And then I close the door so I don't have to see its squalor any more. Perhaps this is a blessing in disguise – at least we can get out of here.

The feeling doesn't stick. Jonah has never walked down stairs before, and with his warped legs, it's no easy feat. After a few steps I wrap him in his blanket and scoop him into my arms. Then with great difficulty, I keep going.

My arms ache by the time we've made it down half the stairs, but I don't stop. Jonah stares around him in awe. Sometimes I forget he's never seen anything outside of our room. His fascination keeps me going. Now I can show him the world. I can see some of it myself too.

The sun is setting outside, and people are still protesting in the square. Packed in tight, they claw at the masses of police officers who try to tame them, screaming obscenities and threats. I set Jonah down on his feet and take his hand as he stares around him. I grab his chin and direct his gaze on me.

"Pay attention for a moment. Whatever you do, don't get lost. Hold my hand at all times. If you can't walk, tell me, I'll carry you. Okay? We have to get far away from the square, it'll be dangerous there. Do you hear me?"

Jonah nods, cringing into himself, and I realize my mistake. He's terrified now. I could kick myself. I've never been good at this soft parenting. I never thought I'd have to prepare him for the world so fast, and now, I'm doing it all wrong. I hug him close to me.

"I didn't mean to scare you. Everything will be okay."

He doesn't believe me. But we don't have time to worry about that. If it's possible, the crowd is getting louder and rowdier. I can see things being thrown at the police, raucous laughter following each direct hit. There are bodies crowded in, overwhelming the men with riot shields and terrified faces. It's hard to feel sorry for them when they're on the wrong side of history, though. They'll survive this, and we won't. As far as we're concerned, they're the enemy.

The crowd surges, pushing the police back no matter how much they try to fend off the citizens. I have a bad feeling in my stomach. This is going to go south very quickly. I want to shout at the protestors to get back, to stop it before they get hurt.

And that's when the gun fires.

People scream, the whole crowd seeming to jump back a meter. More shots begin to fire, endless popping sounds in the air. They've given themselves permission to fight back, and now, people are falling like flies. As more shots sound, people begin to run towards us. A stampede thousands strong.

"Go!" I say to Jonah, starting to run. Jonah's forced to run with me, his arm almost dislocating as I drag him forwards. He stumbles and tries to keep up, but it's clear he won't be able to. We stagger a little further before I pick him up again and carry on running.

People are catching up to us, some shoving past just to get ahead. More gun shots fire and I instinctively duck, sending both Jonah and I hurtling to the ground. I twist to stop Jonah being squashed by me and my back hits the tarmac. The wind is knocked out of me, but I can see feet thundering around us. I have to keep us moving or we're going to die under the crush of a thousand feet, and I'm not ready for that. I scramble to my feet, breathless, and carry on running.

There's nowhere to go. People are pouring out into side

streets and out ahead, but the crowds are still thick. I snap my head back and forth, looking for somewhere to find safety. The gun fire is distant now, a mere popping in my ears, but people are still running. I can't keep going much longer – not while carrying Jonah. I make a snap decision and veer right into the next row of flats.

There's less people out here and the streets are clearer, but with more people coming, we can't afford to stop. I put Jonah down and take his hand again, hoping we can keep up a fairly fast pace. He's slower than me, but he does his best, his eyes darting around us in fear.

And that's when the lights go out.

I hear screams of panic as every streetlamp, every light in every window flickers out. We're thrown into complete darkness. This is it – they've wasted no time in cutting us off completely. They've taken away the power from the poorest areas. They already know that we are not the kind of people that they want to survive this massacre. Now, not even the light from the sky can reach us in this kind of darkness.

It's like we're dead to them already.

Jonah's fingernails dig into my hand and I skid to a stop, pulling him against me protectively. I try to make my eyes adjust, but there's nothing to adjust to. This dark is all consuming. Somewhere high above us, the moon gives off the only light left, but even that is hidden by the buildings.

Someone who hasn't had the sense to stop running slams into me, and I struggle to stay on my feet. As people adjust to the darkness, they begin to fall silent. Because people are beginning to realize that any noise, any movement, is going to draw attention. Attention that could get us killed.

I can hear Jonah breathing. I gently cover his mouth to muffle the sound, planning our next move. We could go inside, but that could easily get us killed. With everyone so on edge, I'm sure people living in the buildings would have no issue with beating us down. We could keep running, but we're blind. But we can't stay where we are. Eventually, someone will find us. Or morning will come, and we'll be exposed.

There are no good options.

I stroke Jonah's hair, trying to breathe quietly. I can't cry now. I can't. I try desperately to see, but there's nothing. Only darkness. I fumble around me for a doorway, and pull Jonah into it with me, sitting on the cold, hard steps. I try to formulate a plan, but nothing comes to mind. I'm terrified to move again, to face the men with their guns or the frightened people abandoned out here. I don't know who will be more dangerous right now. All we can do is wait, and hope for a miracle.

With his face buried in my chest, Jonah falls asleep again. I wish desperately that I had someone who would hold me and let me sleep. But I stay awake, staring into darkness. Listening. Hoping for some kind of a sign of life. Several times, I hear the shuffle of slow footsteps passing us and hold my breath, but tucked away in the doorway, no one even knows we're here.

Time passes, and the sky begins to lighten a little, but still I don't have a plan. This day could hold anything for us. Maybe government officials will roam the streets, shooting anyone who looks at them wrong. Maybe we'll be rounded up like sheep and taken away to extermination camps.

Or maybe things will be more gradual. Less chaotic. Maybe a set of surveys will be mailed to our empty room. Asking questions about family income and qualifications and IQ levels. And if I was there, I'd fill it in, presenting my inadequacy. And then someone would come to the conclusion that I'm unfit for the X drug, come to the house and kill off the final dregs of my family.

I've been wondering for hours if I can cheat the survey somehow. Or maybe I can beg for Jonah's life. He's only a child. But a sickly child at that. What use does this cruel world have for a boy who can't even walk without help? I could tell them he makes me smile. I could tell them he's the sweetest kid. That if they'd only give him a chance, he'd create beautiful art and make people laugh all night long.

That he's good.

And they'd answer me with a bullet to his brain.

I hear the rumble of a vehicle coming down the road and my heart seizes, jumping into my throat. I back further into the doorway's alcove, dragging Jonah with me. My hand fumbles for my knife. Headlights fill the center of the street as a bus comes into view. Fortunately, Jonah and I are still in the shadows. No one's spotted us yet. I take the opportunity to scan the street for signs of life, but there's none that I can see.

The bus stops, and moments later someone gets out and wiggles a torch around the street. They're clearly looking for something. Whether it's people, I don't know. I don't know their motives either, which is worrying. But I don't want to take any chances. We're staying put.

Jonah chooses this moment to wake up and I clamp my hand over his mouth once again. He has the sense to trust my judgment and remains still. I can feel hot tears running over my hand as the person from the bus carries on searching.

The flashlight begins to flicker near us. It jitters up and down the walls and I hold my breath as the light skims over our heads. When the light continues along the wall, I feel as though I can breathe again. We haven't been spotted. Clearly seeing nothing of interest, the figure begins to retreat to the bus.

Suddenly, Jonah lets out a whimper and I freeze once more. The figure turns towards the noise. Within seconds, they're standing right in front of us with their flashlight staring full beam into our faces.

RILEY

I decide after lunch that I'll watch the rest of the fights left over today. Lion always observes them from a special box reserved for V.I.Ps. We're allowed to watch too, but none of us ever really do. Fighting in the Pits provides us with enough bloodshed to last us a lifetime, and some. But today, I want to see what I do from above, as a spectator.

I've done it a handful of times. I watched Elianna's first match after we arrived from the slums. I was scared she wouldn't be able to hold her own, but after she won that first time, I began to relax a little. I decided it wasn't worth the stress of watching every match.

I watched a few of Squid's fights too. Tiger's as well, come to think of it. Lion once told me they put on the best shows. Aside from me, that is. So I wanted to see what all the fuss was about.

But I've never found the fights entertaining. Not like the rich uptown kids do. It's a day out for them. A day of betting and drinking alcohol and roaring in response to the fights with food crammed in their mouths. Me? Once the blood starts spilling, I always have to look away, and I certainly couldn't stomach a meal during. I guess I can't judge when I'm the one providing the entertainment, but I'll never understand how watching kids die can be considered fun.

When I arrive at the viewing box, a fight has already started, but the box is empty, for once. Lion must be working on the advertising for the final fight, which is scheduled for a week today. The room is dark and dank. For a V.I.P box it's, to put it plainly, shit. The only plus to the box is a roof for the days when it rains. There are several wobbly wooden benches lined up by the grubby glass window, and I take one at the front, leaning my chin on my hands.

I recognise one of the kids in the arena. She's good. She's been here even longer than I have. She's got stamina, speed, stealth. It earned her the name Snake. Her hair is shorn short like the girl I fought today. She told me once that in her first fight, a boy grabbed her hair and pulled her back. She said it almost got her killed, and she shaved it all off that night. When I told her I'd miss my hair if I shaved it, she said she'd miss her life if she lost it, and I thought that was a good point, to be honest.

It starts to drizzle outside. I watch Snake scrapping with her opponent as the rain turns the sand pit into slush. The boy Snake is fighting is tall, lanky. But he won't win. Because like me, like Squid, like Tiger, Snake is just too good. This is child's play for her. She's not struggling to win. She's just waiting. It's all for dramatic effect.

A sudden shove sends the boy tumbling to the ground. Snake's boot crashes onto his face and the crowd gasps. I watch their faces. They're frozen in place, eyes fixated. They don't want to miss a second. One woman fumbles for her husband's hand in excitement. She's bet on Snake to win.

I practically feel the crack of the boy's nose as Snake kicks him again. The boy tries to get back up. His hands grapples for his knife. Snake let him keep it, for whatever reason. He thinks he still has a chance. They always do. I respect that. The kids that come to the pit never lose spirit. Even though most of them die in their first battle.

It's all a little predictable. Repetitive. It's rare for kids like me to lose one of the fights. But it gets me thinking…what will happen when Eagle and Bull go together?

I imagine the scene. The two of them stood opposite one another. Feet shoulder width apart as they square up to one another. No wasting time with playful punches and shoving. No. They'll get right in there. Snatch up their knives. Try to end it as soon as possible. But both of them are good. Eagle is sharp – she knows what you'll do before you do. Bull's big and sturdy. She won't go down easy. It's hard to know who has the advantage. For once, I'll watch a fight and have no clue who will walk out alive, and whose body will be dragged away to be burned. It's a scene I don't want to imagine. But somehow, I know I'll be drawn to this box a week today. Somehow, I know I'll watch every second of that match until someone's death seals my freedom.

"I don't think you should go and see her, Phoenix. I heard she's beat up pretty bad," Squid says, picking up one of his boots to polish it.

"What, you think I'm squeamish now? You ain't seen me in the arena?"

"It's different with your friends. You're telling me it won't bother you, seeing her all banged up?"

"Of course it will. But Lion said she's awake now, so she must be okay. I can handle it. I'm not a kid."

Squid shakes his head. "Not in soul, no."

I throw a lone shoe at him. "Give over. Are you coming with me?"

"Better not. Give her my love, though."

"Suit yourself," I say, shrugging on a jacket. "I won't be long."

It's four am. One of my favorite times. When the world's asleep and it becomes my kingdom. Outside is cold, but I stick my hands in my pockets and dash across the courtyard to the infirmary.

There's two people in the ward when I enter. One is a boy I don't recognise. Even if I knew him, the swelling on his face is so damn puffy, I wouldn't recognize him. The other is

Elianna, lying on her back, very still. I can see the shadows of bruises on her face, and her lip is busted open. Her blue paper t-shirt has shifted to reveal that her stomach is bound in bandages like a mummy. She glances up at me.

"You should be sleeping. Won't you be training in the morning?"

"I had a nap. Besides, I don't need to train. I'm already good. One day won't harm me."

Elianna almost smiles, but winces as pain stabs at her. "You're cocky."

I sit on the edge of Elianna's bed. "I'm guessing you missed the newsflash. The Pits are closing."

Elianna tries to sit up in shock, before reclining back in pain. "What? After all we've been through? Why?"

I don't know how to tell her all of this. I already know she's not going to approve of what I've done to save our skin. I take a deep breath.

"There's something going on. A government cull. They're trying to handle the overpopulation crisis…and we're going to be the first to go. They're trying to save the bacon of the rich, so they're giving out some sort of drug to make them stronger, smarter. It's expensive, so Lion knows that no one is going to be wasting money at the Pits…but she's giving us one last chance to walk away with some money. We drew names from a hat. Eagle and Bull are going into the Pit one last time. We'll all split whatever the fight brings in."

Elianna stares at me. "They're going into the Pit…together?"

I nod slowly. Uh-oh. She's going to piece it together. Her eyes widen a little.

"Was this…was this *your* idea?"

I shrug. "I wasn't going to let us walk away with nothing. We wouldn't last a minute. This is our only chance."

"So you're willing to let one of them die for us to live? Riley, how could you agree to this? Those are our friends."

"We all agreed to it. It could easily have been me in there. We all agreed to save each other. Don't look at me like that..."

Elianna shakes her head. "No. This is wrong."

"What choice do we have, Pup? It's this, or all of us get tossed on the street with nothing. Which would you prefer?"

She doesn't have an answer for that. Of course she doesn't. She knows I'm right. Her eyes are watering.

"Knock it out, Pup."

"Don't call me that. We're not some dumb animals, no matter how much you insist on acting like one. I have a real name."

"Alright, Elianna, I get it. You're upset. But crying won't help us. We should be thankful for our lives."

"Thankful?" Elianna splutters. "You've got to be kidding me, Riley. This is not how our lives should be. We should not be fighting every day just to get a meal, a few coins, a few more hours on Earth. We shouldn't be killing our friends just to get ahead!"

I try not to sigh in frustration. "I never said it's ideal, did I? But we could have it a lot worse. We could be dead in a ditch, but we're not. We're alive, and we're going to stay alive for a long time."

"Why are you so calm?"

"Why are you so angry? Is this not what we signed up for? We take our lives into our hands every day. This shouldn't be a shock. I mean, look at you! You're lucky to be alive. And now you never have to do this again. Maybe this could be a chance for a new start."

Elianna's sobbing. She shakes her head, over and over, like she's trying to shake off the rain. "Riley, I swear to God, you're crazy. I love you, but sometimes, I think you don't have a damn heart."

The words nip at me like ticks. I stand up, hiding behind my hair. "You're tired. You didn't mean it. I'll let you rest."

"I did mean it," Elianna mutters, but I'm already walking away. I don't need to listen to this. Not today. She can call me cruel any other day of the week and I wouldn't give a damn. But not after I saved her ass. I've saved *all* our asses. Can't she see that?

I want to kick something hard. It's moments like this, when my anger gets the better of me, that I think about the Pits. At least there, there are no rules about how I can act. I know I shouldn't feel this swelling rage, or get to a level of pissed off where it feels like there's no turning back, but I do. I was born as angry as the red hair on my head. Why shouldn't I be? The hand I've been dealt calls for fury, and it takes everything I have in me not to let it out tonight. Stupid Pup. Stupid Pits. Can't anything ever be simple?

It feels hard to walk away, but I don't want to let it get to me. I've learned not to let tears fall no matter how much they beg, no matter how much they threaten to choke me. But it doesn't mean I'm fine. Just because I don't cry every damn time I get upset, doesn't mean I have no heart, doesn't mean I don't care. I kick the door to the infirmary open, wishing I hadn't visited Elianna. She says I'm cruel. Well she's cold, and serious, and pessimistic, and ungrateful. Every damn day I train that girl. I help her try and get up to speed. I love her like a sister, and I've kept her alive for as far as we go back. She's mad at me for that? Well, I'm mad at her. I'm mad at her for never appreciating a damn thing.

The way I see it, life sucks. It gives you lemons in the basket full. You can either make it into lemonade, or let it turn sour in your mouth until you're so bitter, you can't see something good when it's handed to you. I like to look on the bright side. Because there always is one, even if it doesn't seem like it. My parents died of sickness when I was ten. I spent two years fending for myself on the streets. I fight in a pit for the entertainment of rich assholes who find joy in watching fourteen-year-old girls beat up other kids. The bright side? I'm alive.

See? Easy.

KARISSA

Our wake-up call is a shrill alarm, as usual. I'm on my feet in seconds and ready to go before anyone in my dorm, my jumpsuit neat and tidy while the boys stumble into crumpled garments, fumbling with the buttons and blinking through bleary eyes. When everyone's ready, I march ahead. I want to start this day as I mean to go on, with my head held high. It makes me feel like the leader Captain Strauss wants me to be.

Soldiers from all twelve teams in our sector eat breakfast at the same time. Five am, to be exact. Classes will commence at half past. That gives me some time to figure out how to communicate with my team. If Captain Strauss wants me to lead them, then I first have to get them to like me.

No, not like. Respect.

When we reach the hall, Zach groans at the size of the food line.

"For God's sake. By the time we get to the front, there'll be nothing left."

"Maybe if you got your arse in gear quicker, we wouldn't be last in line every morning," I say. Zach laughs in surprise, almost a little wary.

"She speaks! This is new."

"I guess usually, I just can't get a word in edgeways," I say, raising my eyebrow. Ronan laughs and Zach blushes, before joining in. I allow myself to smile a little as we join the back of the queue. I usually stand alone while the other five huddle together to chat. But today, Zach and Ronan separate themselves off to stand with me. I can see Elliott glaring at me through the corner of my eye, and Minnie seems to be keeping her distance, but I ignore them both. I need to start small and work my way up, which means targeting the betas of the group, not the alphas.

Zach leans on the wall as though he needs it to keep himself standing, while Ronan stands stiff beside him, his eyes wide like an owl. They're chalk and cheese, but best friends, all the same. They come as a pair, so if I want to crack them, it'll be a dual effort.

Zach folds his arms, looking at me like I'm a hard puzzle. Like he's still trying to solve me. That's good. Captain Strauss would like that. It gives me this time to invent who I want to be, who I want them all to see.

"You ready for Pain Endurance? I hear they're upping the pain level a notch this week," Zach asks.

I tend to sit comfortably in the middle of the class for Pain Endurance. Marcia and Ronan always give in first, and Elliott always lasts the longest. Always. He's never been beaten. Most days, he doesn't tell the instructor to stop. He just endures the entire hour, and walks away at the end victorious, in some twisted way. Zach and Minnie never take the class too seriously. They always point out that it's not an inability to endure pain that would kill us if we got shot or stabbed. We'd bleed out, or have to deal with infected wounds. But I want to seem tough right now, so I shrug.

"Bring it on. Maybe I can beat my time this week. I made it to the half hour mark last time."

"I noticed," Zach says, looking me up and down. "I like to keep an eye on how everyone's doing in the team. Assess individual strengths, and such. If I'm going to be Elliott's Second, I need to know those kinds of things."

I raise an eyebrow. "You think Elliott's going to be the Team Leader?"

"Who else would it be?" Ronan says quietly, his eyes trained on the floor. He doesn't seem thrilled at the idea of Elliott having that much control over him. After all, his leadership would be more like a dictatorship. I straighten my back.

"I would be a good team leader," I say before I can stop myself. Zach and Ronan exchange an awkward look and Zach shrugs his shoulders slowly. "Yeah…maybe."

I blush. I've made too sudden a move. I pretend their attitude towards me doesn't bother me. "You think you've got what it takes to be a Second?"

"Well sure!" Zach says, brushing off the awkwardness. "Ronan's definitely not up for it. Marcia would be shit, let's be honest. And just because Minnie flirts with Elliott, doesn't mean he'll pick her. And I guess you and your brother just don't get along enough for him to pick you…"

"No. Really?" I roll my eyes, turning to face the direction of the queue. I can hear the boys shuffling awkwardly behind me.

"Karissa…just so you know. We've got nothing against you or anything. But Elliott is going to be Team Leader and…we need to be on his good side? You know?"

I do know. Whoever becomes Team Leader will be Team Leader for the rest of our lives. Reign as Team Leader only ends if you die or commit a criminal offense. The Team Leader makes all the decisions, and they will call the shots when we finally go to war. They must consult with their Second, and can choose to ask the rest of the team's advice, but ultimately, everything rests on their shoulders. They can discipline their team. They can demote members. Their word is law, basically. And if Elliott has told the team to back away from me, it's no wonder they have.

We have trained so long for a war we still don't fully understand against a land we've never seen, so we need someone who can lead us through the uncertainty of it all.

We need someone willing to make the hard decisions. That could be me, but the others don't see that yet.

That's something I'll have to change.

Zach talks to Ronan for the rest of the queue, and we are greeted at the front by cold porridge and a syringe. We all rush for the table and the others shovel down their breakfast. We have five minutes to eat, but I'm not hungry. I pass my bowl to Zach and he eats it without a second glance. I pick up my syringe, staring at the clear liquid inside. Right now, I'm feeling the effects of an early morning start. Once I inject myself, I'll feel my senses heighten. My pulse will rise. My eyes will adjust. I'll be more alert. Stronger. Smarter. Better. I have five minutes to hope the X drug can enlighten me. Enlighten me on how to beat Elliott to the position of Team Leader.

I push the syringe into my vein. It's easy now. I've been doing it since I was ten. The needle is cold against my skin. I push the X drug into my vein. Already, I can feel its buzz. Feel it's electricity bouncing through the walls of my veins. It zips through my body, snapping every inch of me into life. My body is an obedient soldier, and the X drug is my commander. Within seconds, it's clear what I must do.

I must simply do better.

Pain Endurance takes place in a small room on the West Wing. Each Team has their own room, with six chairs arranged in a circle so we can see each other as we participate. It's supposed to motivate us, and today, I think it will. Marcia crosses the room to take a seat, but I shove past her to get to it first. I want to sit opposite Elliott. I want to watch him as a reminder that I cannot give up.

I must endure for the full hour.

When we've taken our seats, the lights in the room flicker out and we're left in the dark. My eyes only take a few moments to adjust, but in that time, someone comes up behind me and attaches several wires to my head. Wires that will soon deliver excruciating pain to my body.

"Team Nine. I will be observing your efforts today," Captain Strauss' voice booms from a set of speakers somewhere above my head. "I hope to see improvements in all of your times, but as you may be aware, we will be increasing pain infliction to maximum level. I'm sure this will result in some of you dropping out sooner, but as you know, this is all about endurance. The strongest among you will persevere."

I catch Elliott's eye across the room and he smirks at me. I keep my face still. I don't want him to be able to read me. He's an open book to me – he wants nothing more than to beat me. Over and over and over. I embarrassed him last night when we fought. And today, he wants to beat me more than ever. Unfortunately for him, I want to beat him more than ever too, though for very different reasons.

"As usual, the pain will begin for each of you at different times, and will be unexpected. Your timer will begin when you first feel pain. This week, the exercise will be enduring the pain of burns. The pain will simulate exactly what you'd feel if you were burned for real. Should the pain become too much and you wish to give in, press the button on the arm of your chair, as usual. Do you consent?"

"Yes," I murmur, and the others do too. We've learned over the years that we don't really have a choice anyway. It's an illusion that Captain Strauss allows us to have, thinking that we're signing up for this by choice. It's how she got us here in the first place.

"Excellent. Good luck, Team Nine. The exercise will begin soon."

The intercom crackles and then silences. I can hear Marcia's breathing quickening as we wait.

Ronan is first. He gasps, gritting his teeth and clutching at his wrist to try and stop the pain. Minnie follows with a sharp yelp. Marcia is next with a scream that doesn't stop. I keep my eyes on Elliott. I'm determined I won't scream, or yell out. I'm determined to be brave.

And then my skin sets on fire.

It starts in my fingers. Sweat breaks on my forehead. I close my eyes. The ends of my fingers singe. There's no relief. No tap to run my hand under. The fire spreads like my skin is a tree in a forest. Up my arms. Down my torso and legs. And finally, the fire claims my face.

I'm burning alive.

I hear Zach crying out. Elliott is silent, but I'm sure by now the torture has started for him too. My eyes burn like someone's poured acid in them and I claw at them, willing it to stop. Hot tears run down my face, but I can't give in. I won't.

Marcia's screams stop. She's given up. I pull my knees up to my chest, rocking and waiting. It'll be over soon. That's all I can think. It'll be over soon. I hope.

I focus on the X drug in my veins. The thing that makes me stronger. The thing that sets me apart from ordinary people. It'll get me through this. *I can do this. I can do this.*

As I focus, a hush seems to blanket over me. My pain fizzles away until all I feel is a mild tingle on my skin. What's happening? Has my pain become so intense, I've surpassed feeling altogether? Somehow, I don't think so. I've endured worse before. The pain is only just building up. So what's happening?

I open my eyes. The room is silent, and everything seems to be in slow motion. I try to look around, but I feel like I'm underwater. It takes what seems like an age for my head to move a few inches. I can see Zach squirming in his chair, his face contorted in pain, but his legs kick out sluggishly, like he's kicking through mud. Minnie's eyes are closed, passed out from the pain. I see unhurried hands move to her face to unhook her from the wires. She reanimates slowly, moving from her chair.

The whole scene is disorientating. This has never happened to me before. I wonder if the X drug I took this morning was laced with something else, but I don't know of a drug that slows time. Even my thoughts come in a shuffle, like they have all the time in the world to make themselves known.

I decide I don't mind it too much, though. After all, the pain is gone. Even if I don't know why, it's a blessing. This might be my way of surviving the full hour. All I can do is wait. I'm calm as I close my eyes. All I can feel is the tingling on my skin and the pull of time dragging on.

But when my eyes close, the world is white. I'm not in the dark nothingness that usually rests behind my eyelids. In fact, I'm in a room. A white room. It feels familiar, but I've not been here before. I've not left the Institute in eight years, and it certainly doesn't belong here. So what's happened now? Have I teleported somehow? No. I don't believe that. Teleportation isn't possible. Whatever is happening, it's internal. It's all in my head.

The room feels like it's dragging on me. Drawing me in. Somehow, I feel my feet move, though I'm aware that I'm still sitting in the Institute with electrodes attached to my head. Still, I move. I blink. I hear the squeak of my shoes on the clean white floor. The room becomes clearer. I realize it's not a square, but a sphere. And the room isn't white, but in fact like a mirror. A hundred thousand versions of me are heading towards the room's central point.

There's something in the middle of the room. Something shrouded under a black blanket. The color is so dark that it's like it's completely devoid of any hue at all. There's a shape beneath it that I can't decipher. I reach out for it. I want to know what's there. Suddenly, it's the most important thing. It's the only thing in the world I need to know. Forget science, history, math and philosophy. The answer to life, to everything, is right in front of me. All I have to do is –

Cold hands touch my head. My eyes snap open. Someone's pulling away the electrodes on my head. Captain Strauss is standing in front of me.

"Very impressive, Karissa! Did you achieve a meditative state?"

I frown, refocusing on the room. The lights are on. My team is standing behind Captain Strauss, watching me. They look shocked. Impressed.

"Huh?"

"You achieved complete calm, Soldier Gray! I know you're likely a little dazed, but I just wanted to personally congratulate you. You kept your pulse steady, and your brain was releasing all kinds of positive endorphins. A very useful tactic if you're subjected to torture. How did you manage it?"

I don't want to listen to Captain Strauss. I want to be back inside the white room. I want to know what's beneath the blanket. But that world's already slipping away. It's almost as though it was only a dream. Maybe it was.

But a dream has never left me with so many questions.

RAVEN

"Don't kill him," are the only words I can think of to say. I stand and push Jonah behind me, squaring up to the bearer of the torch. But when my eyes adjust, I realize I'm taller than the person in front of me. Much taller, actually. I blink to see if my eyes are deceiving me. But no. The boy in front of me is practically a kid.

"Why would I want to kill a young boy?" the kid reasons. But I don't let my guard down. I hold my knife up and try not to look afraid.

"I don't know you. You could be anyone. You could be working for the government."

"Do I look like I work for the government?"

He doesn't. He barely looks old enough to be out on his own. He's round faced with messily trimmed black hair. His trousers are too long and too wide for his slim hips. But his white t-shirt is splattered with blood. I refuse to stand down, waving the knife and hoping the boy will be scared off. He isn't. He barely even blinks at the gesture.

"You should come with us," he says.

I narrow my eyes at him. "Why?"

"There's a bunch of us holed up at the school uptown. It's well guarded. We plan to make our stand there."

I snort. "A stand against the entire government? Good one."

"Have you got somewhere better to be?"

He has a point. If what he says is true, at least we won't be on our own. Maybe someone will have a clue of how to get to Pink Light City. I still fully intend to get there somehow, and maybe this might be an opportunity to find out more. Maybe I'll even see some familiar faces there. Wren's smiling face comes to mind and my heart aches. This might be my best chance of finding my only friend.

But I don't trust this kid. There's something about him – he seems older than his age. It's disconcerting. He raises a tired eyebrow at me, possessing all the cockiness of a boy on the brink of becoming a teenager.

"I don't have time to wait around for you. Come or don't. But consider this – if I was working for the government, I wouldn't be giving you a choice."

He turns on his heel and begins to walk back to the bus, taking the light with him. "You have a minute to decide before we drive off," he calls over his shoulder.

I have to make a snap decision. I glance back at Jonah. He's desperate. He just wants to be off the streets, somewhere safe. Safety is a feeling we're unfamiliar with, but with everything going on, I can't keep wandering the streets and hoping for a miracle. We have to have more time to make a plan. I gently pick Jonah up, cradling him like a baby.

"I'll keep you safe. It's okay."

I head for the coach and climb the steps with difficulty, shifting Jonah on my hip. Frightened faces peer at us from the other seats. I can hear several children crying.

"Shift your butt. We need to set off," the boy says, peering behind him. I'm blocking the door from shutting. I shuffle down the aisle of seats, and peel Jonah off me. He curls up in a chair, shaking. I shush him and stroke his head until he stops trembling.

The bus trundles forwards for a few miles. We're still near home, but all the streets look the same, and I'm already disorientated. The kid said we're headed to uptown, but the bus is taking an odd route to get there. Picking up more stragglers, I suppose.

Now that Jonah is calmer, I can go and find some answers. I kiss the top of his head and move to the front of the bus to speak with the young boy. If anyone has answers, it's him.

He's sat on the bus steps, surveying the streets. I tap his shoulder.

"So. We got off to a bad start. My name's Raven-"

"I'm Kai. And I'm also busy," he says, staring out the window. I purse my lips and try not to lose patience with the snappy child who somehow seems to be running the show.

"I'll make a deal with you; you answer my questions, I'll keep a lookout for people to pick up."

"Fine. But I don't know why you think I know anything."

It's not encouraging to hear him say it, but I don't know what else I expected. He's just a kid. But I'm not giving up.

"Well...what *do* you know?"

"There's rioting all over the place. Hundreds dead. Maybe thousands," Kai says bluntly. "Of course, the police have no issue with getting trigger happy. Another dead citizen is nothing to them. They know their lives are safe, so long as we all die in their place. But that's not all. The police have got themselves a new weapon."

"Weapon?"

Kai nods, scanning the street. "You'll see."

When he doesn't offer up any more information, I scan the streets, hoping to see what he's talking about. We round a corner and I can suddenly hear the riots. Kai nods to the driver and the bus slows to a stop so we can observe. I see the fires that people have lit, the people standing on top of bins and parked cars. But there are bodies too, and people running away from the scene. At first I think they're survivors trying to escape. But then I notice that they're all dressed the same – in gray jumpsuits. And then I see their faces and my whole body turns cold.

"Step on it," Kai tells the bus driver quietly as the gray jumpsuiters get closer. The driver doesn't need to be told twice. He steps on the gas and I scurry to the back of the bus to watch them attempt to follow us. Their arms windmill as they try to speed up, looking disappointed when they don't catch a bus traveling at twice their speed.

When I retreat back to Kai, he looks amused. "Weird, huh?"

I can't get their expressions out of my head. The ravenous smile they all seemed to bear and the crazed glint in their bloodshot eyes. Dumb expressions, like they lack understanding of what's happening. Thick hair covered their cheeks and foreheads, as though they were animals, not people. Somehow, that was the worst thing about them.

"Are they...human?"

Kai bit his lip. "I'm sure they were once. I have a theory."

"Go on?"

"What letter comes before X?"

"Is that a trick question?"

"Just say it."

"...W."

"And before that?"

I strain to remember the alphabet, one of the few things I learned from my short stint at school. "V...but why does it matter? What are you getting at?"

"The government has this new X drug that they're giving to the rich, right? But they called it the X drug for a reason. They didn't just produce that letter from thin air. And they definitely didn't get the drug right the first time. I think...I think those people are the products of drugs A to W. The ones they messed up. The ones they tested on poor unsuspecting victims who went out to those damned drug trials. They went for the money, but ended up like this. That's my theory, at least."

My skin turns cold. "But...how did they..."

"God knows. But that's the only explanation I can think of."

"How do the government control them? They look...feral."

Kai turns away, looking out into the road. "Maybe they can't. I think the chaos aids them more than it harms them, though. It's scaring people. It's *killing* people."

The thought unsettles me enough that I stop asking questions. These people, these monsters...they look as though they're willing to rip us open with their bare hands. All this time, the government has just been looking for ways to kill us, to get rid of us...and now they're turning us against one another. Those people were probably just like me once. They were desperate for a new start in life, and now, this is what they've been given. It makes me feel cold to my core.

I scan the dark road ahead. Everything still looks the same here; same narrow roads, same buildings as tall as the sky. But now we have no light, and nothing to get up for in the morning, and thousands awaiting a death sentence. There are feral people running around the streets, looking to kill us. I sense a shift in this place. Like the street might suddenly crack down the middle and swallow us whole.

Things are changing.

I'm not sure if I sleep when I return to my seat and close my eyes, but when I open them, we're slowing down. I rub at my eyes, relieved to feel the weight of Jonah's head in my lap after a moment of panic. I squint out of the window to see where we are.

We're uptown — that's clear right away. The buildings here aren't as shabby, and the streets are clean. Plus, I can see the occasional light illuminating a window. It seems the blackout wasn't accidental — it was just selective.

I shuffle from beneath Jonah's resting head and find Kai at the front of the bus. His eyes are drooping, but he's still awake. I nudge him and he glares at me — I'm clearly the most irritating passenger on the bus, in his opinion.

"What?"

"Where's the school?"

"You're looking right at it."

At the end of the road, an enormous building looms over the rest of the road. This must be the main road in town – we've already passed several shops and business buildings. But the school trumps all the rest. It's almost entirely made of glass, and is so tall I can't see the top from inside the bus.

The area here isn't so dense, but there are more cars than I've ever seen before, several of them even on the move. But not the practical kinds of cars we have downtown for transport – these cars are made for speed and style; scarlet, magenta, cobalt and emerald vehicles studding the road like jewels. It's been four years since I've been anywhere within miles of uptown, and so much has changed. Somehow, it's become bigger and better. It seems crazy to me that so many people are living in squalor and yet in this part of town, people have everything they could ever need and more.

I press my face against the glass to look at the school. Logan would have studied here. I used to beg him to describe uptown; a place I'd never have a chance to properly explore. And now, all of his descriptions are coming to life before my eyes.

As we approach the school, it's clear that it's heavily guarded. The walls surrounding the schools almost look as though they were made as a fortress, and now they're lined with makeshift soldiers, carrying various weapons from baseball bats to guns. It's amazing how quickly defenses were thrown together overnight. Where they got the guns from, I don't know, but I feel safer already.

By the main gate, a group of women stand, guns trained suspiciously on the bus. Kai jumps out of the bus and jogs to speak to them. One of them nods at whatever Kai said and signals for someone to open the gate to let us through. Kai acts as an usher and the bus creeps forwards into the parking lot.

As we come to a halt, Kai gets back on the bus. "Alright, everyone. Last stop."

As I allow people to pass me, I notice how many more people have got on the bus since we boarded. Jonah's the last person to hobble down the aisle and as we exit, I see that we're not the only bus load. Several other buses are hurrying people off, and then turning around to head out again.

"Raven, I'm scared," Jonah whispers. I kiss the top of his head.

"We're safe here. I promise you. Just stay close to me."

I spot Kai among a group of people. There's a woman holding him close and kissing the top of his head. I lead Jonah over to him and tap his arm. He peeks over the woman's shoulder.

"You again?"

"Yeah, sorry..."

The woman pulls away from Kai, smiling at me. "Kai's overtired, ignore his grumpiness. Would you like me to take you inside and get you settled?"

I blush, feeling like a child, not a competent seventeen year old. But I nod gratefully and the woman, who introduces herself as June, calls the attention of everyone in the area before leading everyone inside.

Inside is chaos. People are milling everywhere; passing each other sideways on the stairs to make room, squashing into lifts so they can shoot up to different floors and get settled. I keep tight hold of Jonah's hand, scared of losing him. Kai's mother ushers us all towards the lift and my heart skips a beat. I've never been in one before – even when I went to watch Ma's shows, we were told to take the stairs to the top floor to keep us separate from the rich folk who attended Alec Golding's parties. Now, I'm not sure I even want to get inside the metal box, but I don't have much choice.

Inside the lift, it's suffocatingly hot. Jonah and I are some of the first to get in, and endless streams of people seem to pile in after us, crushing us against the wall of the elevator. I feel sick as the doors close and it lurches upwards, my legs wobbling. Bodies shift. There's not enough oxygen in this lift for everyone. I watch the top of the lift, where there's a screen that tells us which floor we're passing. Three, four, five. I can feel a sweat breaking on my forehead. Eleven, twelve, thirteen. I close my eyes, praying I won't be sick. Then all of a sudden, I hear the doors open and everyone spills out. I sigh, taking in a lungful of air and trying to pretend the experience didn't scare me.

As I exit the lift, I realize we're essentially in a huge classroom. All of the desks have been pushed to the sides of the room to accommodate for all of the refugees. And there's hundreds of them. It's like being back in the marketplace. Some people have brought possessions, but the majority of people are sitting with only their family and the clothes on their backs. I'm suddenly grateful that Jonah and I have blankets, at least. June comes over to us, patting Jonah's curls affectionately.

"Find a space where you can. I know it's cramped, but it's safe here. You can get some rest, and everything will be okay in the morning."

I want to believe her. Desperately. I know we're automatically safer in the richer part of town, where most of the people living here are going to be eligible for the X drug. They have no need to be rioting here, and the police will be concentrating their efforts elsewhere. We blend in in that sense, but eventually, we'll be figured out. So I believe we're safe – for now. But in the morning, I'll come up with a new plan.

There's a space between a few families big enough for Jonah and I. A mother with a little girl tucked under her arm greets us with a tired smile. It makes me feel a little more comfortable about sharing the room with so many strangers.

"Are you hungry?" I ask Jonah. I untie my makeshift sack and offer him a cup of soup and a hunk of bread. He tears at the bread, a little soup dripping on his chin. I catch the woman staring at him, her lips dry. I immediately feel guilty. I don't want to have to share with everybody in the room, or there'll be none left for Jonah and I, but something makes me pass a chunk of bread to the woman. She smiles. Her teeth are crooked and rotten behind her flaky lips. She thanks me, and feeds crumbs to her child.

Time passes. It begins to lighten outdoors. Jonah's asleep again, the flask of soup clutched to him for warmth and a blanket draped over him. I fidget, too alert to sleep. Eventually, I decide I must explore before I go crazy. I ask the woman next to us to watch Jonah for me. In thanks, I lend her my blanket, which she cocoons around her child.

With people still streaming in and out of the elevator, I decide the stairs are a safer option – and a less scary one. I climb and climb and climb until my legs ache. I pass classrooms filled to the brim with refugees, glossy canteens where volunteers are preparing a makeshift breakfast, abandoned teacher's lounges that smell of coffee. I climb ten floors, twenty. I lose count. The floors get quieter the further up we go. I start to get tired and abandon the stairs to explore the floor I'm on. I push through the heavy double doors to see what this level has to offer.

I'm in the biggest gym I've ever seen. The room is filled with equipment; treadmills, punching bags, yoga mats, rowing machines, weights of various sizes. Logan's family apartment had a gym, but it was nowhere near this lavish – it was only a small room, with enough space for Logan's weights, treadmill and punching bag. We used to spend hours there while Ma and Pa worked their night shifts. Logan said I had potential – I could fight. I was much better than he was. I guess since I'd learned to take a few punches in the rough end of town, I'd learned how to throw them too.

I could run faster and longer than he ever could, too. Once or twice, he took me up to the pool on the roof of the building and I'd delve into cool waters, opening my eyes and swimming through the calm blue. I grew strong – stronger than that little rich boy – until I beat him in nearly every fight. I'd give anything right now to be play fighting again with my old friend, but I left that life behind a long time ago.

I walk into the room. I'm drawn to the red leather of the punching bags – it's familiar. I stroke the material. It's coarse against my hands. I ball my hands into fists, imagining Logan stood opposite me. If I concentrate, I can see him standing on the opposite side of the bag, his sweaty blonde hair plastered to his face.

"Go on. Show me what you've learned," he says. I get my feet moving, bouncing to and fro. My fist slams against the bag. Once. Twice. Without gloves, the leather hurts, but I'm no stranger to a little pain. I've broken a few noses in my time, but I've broken my fingers more times than I can count.

"You can do better than that," Logan reminds me. And I can. I hit the bag again. I dodge an invisible retaliation. My arm swings out again and again. My knuckles are bleeding a little. I don't care. It feels good to be lashing out. The past day flashes before my eyes. My anger, my fear. I punch it all out. I finish up with a kick, the bag swinging as I stumble back, panting. I'm sweating, breathing hard.

"Still got it, Raven Verona."

It takes me a moment to realize the voice isn't in my head. I stare across the gym. Leaning against the doorframe with his hands in his pockets is the ghost of my past. His smile sends a shiver down my spine.

"Long time no see," Logan Golding says.

RILEY

I can't bloody sleep. I'm not the best of sleepers anyway. There's something about never feeling completely safe that makes you wary about closing your eyes. But it's sunrise and I'm thinking about everything that's going on in the world. In less than a week, I'll have to leave here. The others too. We'll be thrown back on the streets to figure out how to survive while the government cook up some plan to kill us off. But I like to think I'm a cockroach – a bit gross at times, but kind of invincible. I've survived a lot. I mean, I'm not saying I can survive being hit by a bullet, but I'm a master at dodging them.

It's not that that worries me so much. I don't need a bed or food handed to me on a silver platter. I've lived without it before; I'll do it again. No. It's more about the people I'm leaving. Squid and Pup are like siblings to me. But I can't take them with me. Because out there, the odds are worse than us fighting in the Pits. We're good, but we're not that good, and we're easier to find in groups. It's safer to go alone, so people might underestimate me as a small, innocent child. That's how I survive.

And then I don't have to watch them all die.

I don't trust our world. It takes more than it gives. I

should know. Bam, Ma's sick. Bam, Pa loses his job and can't afford medicine for Ma. And then he gets sick too. Bam, bam, bam. Can't say my life has no drama. Bam. They're both dead and I need to figure out how to survive on my own. The way I see it, the world owes me a favor or something, but I'm not counting on that. So that means I need a plan. And a good one.

I sit up in bed. Everyone else is still asleep. It's pretty dark in here, but I can see just enough to fumble for my bag and spill my possessions out in front of me.

I don't have much. I never did. I guess being poor doesn't allow for being a materialistic girl. But I picked up some pretty nifty stuff. I've got some money I stole and the ration card I got forged back when I lived in the slums. There's an array of knives I've collected over the years. An empty water bottle. The wedding bands Ma and Pa once wore. I did consider selling them, but I guess I'm sentimental. Besides, they're made of tin. Worth very little.

But that's not what I'm looking for. I've got a map somewhere in here. I ripped it from a billboard back in the city center. It led me here – maybe now it'll get me someplace else of use. I squint at the page, looking for places that seem familiar. There's Pink Light City, of course, but it's risky going there. It's like me strolling into uptown. I don't look remotely like I could belong there. I don't exactly blend in anywhere, but there, they'd take one look at my crooked teeth and wild red hair and run a mile. I'd be grubby, too. People who can afford showers don't like to spend time with those who can't. Like the smell will catch or something. If I showed up like that in Pink Light City, they'd probably shoot me on the spot.

There's always space for one more in the slums, I suppose. Don't have to pay rent either. And you don't have to walk far to find a slum. There's one right outside the Pits. People sit outside the grounds and beg for pennies as the rich hurry past them to spend their day gorging and betting. I've often watched them from the top of the stands and wondered if I could throw food down to them. But if I lined their stomachs, mine would stay empty. That's how I push off the guilt. Besides, they tend to be the fresh meat in the Pit – the outsiders who lose to kids like me. They come hoping for glory, hoping for a new life, and then by the end of the day, they're watching the business end of my knife disappear into their bodies. There's no point saving them only to have to kill them.

I could go back to where I was born. Watermouth smells like fish and salt air. Most people lived in makeshift houses made from wood that rotted away in the rainy season. Those who are lucky enough to have boats stay out on the water and try to pretend that they don't get seasick. I liked it there, for whatever reason. Felt like home. But when Ma and Pa died, I sold our hut so I had money for food for a few weeks. So long as I rationed the rations, anyway. It seems like an option. Maybe I could buy a boat. Or make one. Take off to sea. I could live my life out catching fish in a net like Ma taught me. Out at sea, no one would have reason to want to hurt me. I wouldn't be doing no harm. My finger hovers over it on the map. I trace the curve of sea against land. I think home is a good plan. It'll take time to get there. It's half a world away. But I've done it before. I can do it again.

"What you doing, little lady?"

I look up. Squid's standing by my bed, looking at the map. I cross my arms.

"Nowt."

Squid raises an eyebrow. "Nowt? So you're not planning your escape route? Without me?"

I roll my eyes, not sure what to say. Squid sits down next to me, looking at the map.

"I used to live in Bridgwater," he tells me. He jabs at it on the map. I cock my head to the side. He didn't live too far from me. A dozen or two towns over, maybe. I smirk. It's fitting that Squid comes from the seaside.

"I never knew that."

"Course not. Never told you, did I? My Ma lives there

still. Far as I know anyway. If I could send her something, I would, but we ain't making money here. But she'll be okay. She's a tough one. She works damn hard. You'd like her."

I chew on my thumb. This is the most Squid's ever told me about his life before the Pits. We always kept our lives secret. The lives we used to live, at least. I don't really know what to stay to that.

"You could come with me. I bet you'd be a dab hand at fishing. It's long hard work, but I know you ain't scared of that. We might be safer, by the coast. Got somewhere to run to if things turn upside down. Or swim, rather."

My thoughts exactly, Squid. It occurs to me that if we're headed in the same direction that maybe it would make sense to go together. But there's still the fear of losing him to cope with. I wonder what to do. I can't say no without him asking why. He'd try to persuade me differently. I sigh, pointing at Watermouth.

"I've got a stop I want to make on our way," I tell him. He grins, ruffling my hair.

"Wherever you want, kid. You know, people used to travel for pleasure. We could plan a route. See some cool stuff."

"Yeah. Cool," I say. I don't mention that I don't plan to stick with him. Come next week, after the fight, I'll sneak out alone. It'll hurt him. But for now, I let him get excited.

I don't want to hurt him until I have to.

RAVEN

I want to scream and kiss him and cry and ask if he's real and kick him and go out of my mind. Four years apart and he's acting like he saw me yesterday. I want to go wild, but I don't. Instead, I take a step back, half hidden behind the punch bag. He raises an eyebrow at me, stepping into the room.

"You got nothing to say? That's not like you."

"How would you know? You haven't seen me in four years," I say. I mean to sound angry, but my voice is barely a whisper. Logan's face holds its smile.

"Well, whose fault is that?" he asks. I turn towards the window so that I don't have to look at him, but I can see his reflection. He approaches slowly, his hands still dug in the pockets of his neatly pressed trousers. Ever cool, ever collected.

"When I found out the refugees were coming here, I came right away. I came to find you," he said, joining me at the window. I look to see if I can read his face. I always used to be able to. But now he's so poker-faced, I don't even recognise him. I shift on my feet.

"Why?" I whisper. Logan shakes his head.

"Why? Why? Because you're the best friend I ever had, Raven. I missed you every single day. My father wouldn't tell me where you live. Every weekend, I go downtown and hope to glimpse you at the markets. I skipped school some days just hoping to find you. I've been searching for you for years. Since the last time I saw you."

The last time I saw you. I remember that night all too well. Maybe Logan doesn't know what happened. It would be typical of Alec to keep the truth a secret from him. But this is a man I don't know anymore. I have no way of knowing whether to trust him. I press both my hands against the window, leaning against it to catch my breath. Logan leans his back against the window. I can feel him looking at me. I hope he can't see my blush.

"Anyway, I thought I would find you up here. You were always fascinated by the gym back home. I never saw anyone go so hard on a punchbag as you."

"I had to learn to fight," I mutter. "I wouldn't call protecting myself fascination."

"You can't deny you loved the rush. You were always so feisty."

He's looking at me like he knows me. He's talking like he knows me. But we're strangers now. When you don't see someone for four years, change is inevitable. He's the same, but different. He's bulked out and he's broader than he was. He's taller. Much taller. I barely reach his shoulders. But his face has grown older, and that's the biggest change. His face isn't creased with laughter lines anymore. His eyes are dulled, as though rich boys have such a hard life. I regard him coolly.

"What do you want, Logan? I'm here. You've found me. Now what?" I ask. His face crumples a little.

"I…I wanted to know that you're okay."

I take a step back from him. "Well. Now you know. I'm doing just fine."

Logan's face breaks completely. I'm suddenly seeing the boy I knew – sensitive, kind, emotive. Now that he's back, I feel guilt. I feel pain.

"Why are you doing this to me? Raven, after all this time…you don't even want to look at me. Why?"

I have to look away so he doesn't see tears prick my eyes. I start to storm away. "Maybe you should ask your father."

Parties at the Golding household were lavish to the extreme. Alec would spend all the money he made on the delicacies that made him look the richest; large cuts of red meat, pots full of steaming vegetables and crusty white bread; emerald jellies, crumbly pastries and rose iced cakes, all followed by circular little mints, shots of spirits and little blue pills that made people's faces sag and the laughter flow when nobody was even talking. Our family was always invited to the parties, though we didn't fit in there. After all, Ma was the star of the show.

Entertainment was common at parties of the rich. Alec enlisted my mother as his own personal singer when he heard her singing while working in the baker's van one day. He promised her money and expensive clothes and food to die for, but she took the job only to put food on our table.

And at first it was good. I loved going to those parties. I was at an age where my curiosity with boys and girls was beginning to show. I'd go into the room and see endless possibilities for romance with the rich kids. But it was always Logan that caught my eye the most.

Alec Golding smoked like a chimney and always sat in the dining area during his parties, where the tea-time entertainment was. That's where Ma would perform. Alec would let her pick clothes from his deceased wife's wardrobe. My mother would don dresses with silver tassels and skirts that fanned out when she twirled, her face smothered in pastes and glitter. It was supposed to make her look beautiful, but I never liked it. The sight of her scared me. She didn't look like herself.

But back then I didn't overthink it. I'd sit with Logan and his friends, Lark and Theodore, to watch the shows. Theodore was good company with his expressive eyes and gentle demeanor, talking often about books he'd read and music he'd listened to. Lark was a terrible flirt and way too loud for my liking, but he was still part of the gang.

But my eyes were always drawn to Logan.

Maybe that's why I overlooked how much I hated his father. Alec would recline into his purple velour chair and prop his feet on a table, a cigarette dangling from his yellowed fingers. His eyes would smother my Mum. He'd lick his lips as she swayed in time to the music. The other men there were just the same. It made me feel sick. And it made my father retreat to the buffet table to pour himself a drink.

"Looking good," I'd say every time I saw Logan, his neck choked by a bow tie. And he'd smile a half smile, not quite pleased to be there, but pleased to be in my company. I knew how to make him laugh, so I would. He was always so depressed at those parties, but I know that at the time, we were one another's saviors.

Then we'd retreat from the party and go running up to the rooftops, or to the gym where we'd play on the apparatus. Sometimes, Lark and Theodore would join us, but mostly, Logan snuck us off so we could be alone.

Logan's room was a minefield of toys when we were younger. As we grew up, they were replaced by piles and piles of books. Sometimes, at three am when the parties were winding down, we'd just sit together and he'd read to me, our backs rested against his pillow. It all suited me just fine.

It was only as I got older I understood what was happening. I'd catch Alec cornering Ma after each show, his fingers brushing her skin as he leant close, whispering in her ear. I'd watch her squirm, but smile. But after Alec's chauffeur took us all home in the dead of night, I'd hear her crying on Pa's shoulder while he poured them both a drink. Those nights I'd curl up next to Jonah and wish Ma would get another job. One that wouldn't hurt her so much.

April. Four years ago. Alec threw a spring ball. It was by far the most expensive, most talked about party of the year. Everyone heard about it – even in downtown. The theme was gold, to match the family name, and Alec had Ma and I fitted with gold silk gowns that fell just past our knees.

For the first time, Pa wasn't invited.

For once, Logan was already at the party when I arrived. I guess he'd been dragged there early for the big event. Lark wolf-whistled me as I approached the boys.

"Well, someone scrubs up well," Lark said with a huge grin. Theodore slapped his arm.

"Ignore him, Raven. You always look lovely."

I shrugged. "I couldn't really care less about what Lark thinks," I said, glancing at Logan. His was the only approval I craved. There was a slight blush on his cheeks as he looked at me.

"You look amazing," he told me. Lark was sniggering behind him, but as I reached for Logan's hand and pulled him up to dance, the smirk was wiped right off his face.

His hand was tentative on my waist as he guided me around the floor. It was the first time that I noticed his hair wasn't yellow, but gold, like his name, and his eyes weren't just blue, they were the color of the sea and the sky and those little blue pills everyone took at these parties. Lark and Theodore watched us like proud parents, smiling to themselves as they realized that the night would be etched on our hearts forever.

Or so I thought.

Ma sang beautifully that day. Her eyes were alight, rimmed with gold glitter. I watched her and knew I was feeling pride, even if I didn't think Alec's parties were the right place for her to sing. Her lyrics were thick and sweet like honey, and everyone was lapping it up, intoxicated by her and the pills and the spirits. Everyone's eyes were glazed over, almost tired, as they danced.

But when I looked up at Logan, his eyes were perfectly clear. He was watching me, smiling. I remember how I trembled then, intimidated by the beauty of him. My hands were gripped on the back of his jacket, holding myself close to him. Logan took a hand from my waist to tip my chin towards him. His eyes searched for an answer to an unspoken question. *Can I kiss you?*

I wanted to say yes.

The song ended, and so did the night. For me, at least. The audience fell into lazy applause, their hands struggling to meet each other. Logan and I began to clap too, dropping our hands away from one another. As the audience began to retreat to the door, I gently touched Logan's hand. I wanted to go and see Ma.

"I'll be back," I promised. I pushed through the crowd, trying to spy her on the stage. I concluded that she must have gone to collect her things.

I found her in her dressing room – Logan's mother's room – but she wasn't alone, and she was crying. I hid behind the door frame, listening.

"I've given you everything," Alec growled. "You'd be nothing without me."

"Alec...I came here to work. That's what you offered me. A job."

"And now I want more."

There was a long pause. I heard Ma take a shuddering breath. "You can't have it."

Silence again. I could hear her crying, even as my heartbeat roared in my ears. I wanted to go to her. I didn't quite understand at the time what he was trying to force her into, but I knew she was in danger just by being there with him. And yet my feet stayed rooted to the ground.

"You're damn ungrateful," he growled at her. "You made the wrong decision tonight. Your child could have had a life like this. You've failed her."

I felt sick. I wanted to tell him he didn't know a thing. Ma had given me everything she could. She worked her fingers to the bone for me. And at what price to herself? I'd only find that out later.

Then she retreated from the room, wiping her face. She caught sight of me and grabbed my wrist.

"We have to leave."

"But-"

"Please don't argue, Raven. We're walking home."

"I didn't say goodbye to Logan…"

Ma took my face in her hands. The gold glitter smeared on her face seemed unnatural now, wrong. There was fear glistening with gold in her eyes.

"You won't be seeing him again, sweetheart. These are not good people, do you hear me? We have to go."

The next day, Ma told us she would no longer be working for the Golding family. She said that we'd be okay – she'd get another job. Not one that paid as much, but we'd be okay. But she wasn't okay. Pa was barely speaking to her. She'd lost her passion. She'd lost the ability to support our family. It became too much.

In the end, I know Alec Golding was the reason Ma jumped.

There is no hint of a smile on Logan's face anymore. My recollection of that night seems to have aged him ten years. Sometimes when I think of what happened then, I wonder how Logan can be related to a man like him. Logan would never try to force a woman to be with him. He has always been so kind and patient and loving in a way his father never could be. And yet, when I look at him now, I can't quite separate him from his father.

"Raven…I'm so sorry. I had no idea why your mother left her job. I knew how my father felt for her…but I didn't think he'd give her an ultimatum like that."

I turn away from him. I can't talk about this right now. My throat is closed shut and I can feel tears pricking my eyes. I've lost so much. I haven't given myself an opportunity to grieve for Pa either, but I'd planned to brush it all under the carpet. I know I have to keep it together now more than ever, for Jonah's sake and my own. But ten minutes with Logan and I've come undone. Everything I've ever felt is pushing for attention.

I'm not prepared for this.

"It doesn't matter now. What's done is done." I glance up

at Logan with tears in my eyes. "You can't change the past."

I think I must have slept a while. When I open my eyes, the room where I'm camping out is buzzing with noise and Jonah is gone. I search around frantically, terrified of losing him.

"He's playing with the other kids," the woman next to me says with a reassuring smile. She points to the center of the room. Some girls are trying to teach Jonah some elaborate kind of clapping game, and he's trying to keep up, his face knotted in concentration. The sight makes my heart swell. He's never played with other kids before. I never thought about how much that sucks until now. I head over to Jonah and he smiles sweetly at me.

"Hey Raven, I made some new friends!"

"That's great," I say, kissing the top of his head. I can't drag him away now. Not when he seems so happy. Besides, I need time to think and maybe I should do that alone. Do we stay here? Is it safe? Can I commit to staying here if Logan is going to stay too? If Alec shows up looking for him then I don't know what I'll do. "If you stay here with your friends, do you promise to be good? I'm trusting you…"

"Okay," Jonah says, beaming. I hug him close, not wanting to let go. But now that it's morning, I have to figure out what's happening. Which means finding whoever is in charge of the operation here. If I'm going to stay here I want to be sure that I'm in good hands. As nice as it is that someone has taken charge here, I won't be satisfied until I know more.

I explore a few floors of the school, asking around for a figure of authority, but everyone seems to be just as clueless as me. I check one of the canteens and find almost two hundred people crowded in there, but when I ask around, no one seems to know who is in charge.

So instead, I hunt for Kai. He seems like my best bet for finding order. He seemed to have some understanding of the system yesterday. I almost walk straight past him when I arrive on the bottom floor of the building. He's holding a bunch of blankets and scurrying for the elevator.

"Hey!" I yelp. He keeps walking but whips his head around to look at me.

"You again."

"Yeah…I want to find out more about what's happening. I want to know what I can do to help."

"You want to help?" Kai shoves his stack of blankets into my arms. "Take these to floor thirty-four. Then go outside and get more."

"Where's all this stuff coming from?"

"You ask a lot of questions. How am I meant to know?" Kai says, already halfway down the corridor. "A private investor, I guess."

Someone rich, he means. But there's not one person here who is rich. That's why we're here. So where is all this stuff coming from? As I look around, I realize that others are carrying supplies. Crates of fruit. Threadbare pillows. Oddly, spare shoes. It's a bizarre sight. Somehow, someone is creating organization in the chaos.

I do as Kai requested and take the blankets upstairs, gritting my teeth as the elevator lurches upwards. Then, I hurry outside to see if I can make sense of everything.

Outside, there are several large lorries being unloaded. They're familiar to me only from seeing them at the market. One of the lorries is still completely full, cardboard boxes filling it right to its ceiling. I look around to see who looks important enough to be running the operation. Basically, someone who looks like they're part of the rich boy's club. Neat clothes, good shoes, clean faces.

Then, of course, I spot Logan.

He's not alone, but I'm relieved to see Alec isn't with him. Of course - I should've known - Theodore and Lark are with him. They always did follow Logan wherever he went. It would also explain some of the supplies here. Lark's family manufactures clothing for the middle class, hence the shoes. Theodore's adopted parents have a pharmaceutical business, so of course they're rich. Maybe they're even expanding their fortune with the arrival of the X drug.

The three of them together are a triad of good fortune, so why are they here? If they're willing to risk everything to help the poor then they must be really committed. After all, they could be applying for the X drug right now. Something tells me Lark is here because Logan is, and Theodore's conscience has saved him from selfishness. Whatever their excuses are, I guess I should be thankful.

June is among the people Logan is standing with, and she's holding a clipboard. Logan is the last person I want to speak to after our interaction in the gym, but he knows what's going on for sure. I have to go over there.

I decide I know enough of the group to have a reason to speak with them. I march over, and Logan spots me almost right away. His mouth twitches like he wants to smile, but he doesn't quite manage it.

"Well I never," Lark says as he spots me. "Raven Verona...I thought you'd disappeared off the face of the earth."

"Thought or hoped?" I respond sweetly. He grins at me, his freckled cheeks dimpled as they always were. Since I last saw him, he's grown much taller, but his auburn hair still shines with gel and his lips are still constantly smirking. Theodore steps forward and pulls me into a hug.

"It's good to see you," he tells me. "I was worried when you stopped showing up at the parties. Have you been well?"

"As well as I can be," I say with a blush as we pull apart. I've always been struck by how handsome Theodore is. His dark skin and kind eyes are enough to make most girls swoon. He's dressed well in fitted pants and a clean white shirt, but he doesn't have the same vibe as most rich boys. He grew up in poverty, just like me. He knows his own privilege now and he's never been one to abuse that.

"Hey, Raven," Logan says gently. "You disappeared last night."

"Sorry...I needed some time," I say truthfully. He nods a

little uncomfortably, his hands buried in his pockets and his shoulders tensed.

"I understand. What are you doing out here?"

"I'm looking for answers. I want to know what's going on here. Who is running this whole thing, where this stuff is coming from...but I guess you guys are responsible for that in part."

"Some of it. Logan got us together for the donations...but June and Ellis have been at the heart of it all," Theodore says, modestly stepping to one side to show June and a woman with pouty lips and limp hair deep in conversation. I step forward, hoping to speak to them.

"Excuse me. Can you tell me more about what's going on here? I'm here with my family and I need to know how safe it is to stay."

The woman with pouty lips looks me up and down in disapproval. "Why, do you think you've got somewhere better to be?"

"Ellis!" June says in a scalding tone. She turns to me. "In truth, we're doing our best, but it's going to be hard here."

"That's why I'm asking. There are hundreds of people here. We're going to need a lot of supplies. What's the plan?"

"Why don't you allow the adults to handle this?" Ellis says condescendingly. I fold my arms around myself. I think of how Pa handled this situation, and I know that I can't trust someone just because they're older. It doesn't actually make them any wiser.

"Allowing adults to handle things has never turned out well for me," I say, keeping my voice level. "That's exactly why we're in this mess in the first place. So don't patronize me. I want to know what's going on, and I want to help."

Lark sniggers and Ellis sucks in air through her nose. June looks unsure how to react, shifting on her feet. Logan smiles.

"The truth is, Raven, we're not too sure of ourselves right now," he admits. "I've tried to bring in as many supplies as I can from my father's warehouse, but they won't last us long. Not with the sheer amount of people here."

"Logan!" Ellis hisses. "You can't go around saying things like that. You'll create widespread panic, you foolish boy."

"I don't think anyone here is particularly calm. Their lives have been turned upside down," Logan reasons. "Besides. I've known Raven for a very long time. I owe it to be honest with her."

After our earlier conversation, the comment makes my face burn. I refuse to look at him, staring at Ellis instead. She purses her lips even more like she's tasted something sour.

"Well. If you must know, we have plans to attempt self-sufficiency," she says. I raise an eyebrow.

"How do you expect to manage that? Bring in a bunch of rich kids to buy everything for us?"

Ellis blushes. June brushes my arm gently.

"I know it sounds silly. We know it won't be easy. But right now, we don't have any other options. We figured that if we split ourselves off, became a separate state which the government isn't responsible for, then they have no reason to want us dead. We'd have to work quickly. Try to grow some basic vegetables and such. We can possibly rear some animals in the future for slaughter. The rest will very much come down to what we can steal at the start. While the rioting is still happening, we have an opening to get supplies without much consequence."

"But if we do this, the rest of the city will be forbidden property," Theodore explains. "If we declare ourselves as a separate state then we'll lose our rights in the rest of the country, not just the city. We could be killed for entering. It's all very risky. That's why we're keeping this all on the down low."

I shake my head. "How long will it take to grow food? What is there to steal when no one has anything? I don't see how any of this can work..."

June smiles sadly. "We know it's not ideal. We know it's not a good plan. But we owe it to ourselves to try. If we don't do this, what else can be done? We'll be killed. We're of no use, in their eyes. This is an option that lets us fight against the system. If by some miracle we can do this, then we'll have saved ourselves. Isn't that worth a try?"

"You have to realize, this is the only option we have right now. Until we come up with something better. It's a case of surviving until we can form a real plan," Logan says. "Do you still want to help?"

The idea is ludicrous. But is mine much better? Wander aimlessly across the country until I stumble on something good? At least here, we have some protection. People with guns, anyway. It's the better of two bad ideas. I sigh, shrugging. "Well. It's better than just sitting around. What can I do to help?"

"Why don't you and I deliver some of this food to the canteen?" Logan asks. He looks hopeful that I'll say yes. He clearly wants time alone with me. Not that I have much of a choice right now. I nod and his face lights up.

"Let's go. We'll reconvene at one pm," Logan says to the others in the group. They all nod in agreement and scatter across the parking lot, leaving Logan and I alone. Theodore pulls Lark away by his arm while Lark grins and watches me and Logan over his shoulder.

I can feel Logan watching me too. I blush, feeling embarrassed for how I acted last night. I sway on my feet, unable to meet his eye.

"I just-"

"No, I just-"

We titter quietly at our nervousness. I finally find the courage to look up at him.

"I just want to say I'm sorry for last night. I took my anger out on you and walked away...but you're not the one I'm mad at."

Logan shifts, looking away from me. "I know. Well, I hoped. After we spoke...I confronted my father. He admitted that he asked your mother to be with him, but he wouldn't admit that he did anything wrong. I believe everything you told me...that he fired her for saying no to him. Raven, if I had known...I would have understood why you never came back. I just wish you'd told me. You know I would've been on your side."

He's right. I said I would come back for him, and I never did. I owe him an explanation for why. He deserves that much.

I close my eyes. I don't like reliving what happened. But for this purpose, I have to. I give myself a few seconds to prepare. Then I open my eyes again, meeting Logan's curious gaze.

"Last year...she killed herself. Pa was angry with her. Even after she left a job she loved, even after she rejected your father...he was angry. Maybe jealous. Maybe mad that she couldn't provide for us anymore." I swallow back tears, shaking my head.

"For three years, I watched her fade. And I knew that was on him. And you're his son. That was a hard connection to deal with. And that's why I told myself I'd never see you again. And I know that's not your fault, but that's how it was."

Logan shakes his head, his eyes glistening. "I'm so sorry. I'm so sorry he hurt you. And her."

Tears beg to squeeze out of my eyes, but I try to keep myself composed. I lower my head so Logan can't see my face. "Pa's gone too. He jumped last night. After the announcement."

Logan looks horrified. "Raven, I-"

I wave away his apologies and sympathies. It's not what I need. "No. It's better this way. He caused more harm than good. Jonah's safer without him. I can take better care of him than Pa ever could. I just want you to know. The whole picture. Now that I'm being honest."

Before I can stop him, Logan rushes me into a hug, gripping me tight against him. It's been so long that it should feel wrong, but it feels good. To have someone hold me up, to show me some familiarity that doesn't bring me pain. I'm used to it being the other way around. I rest into him. I know this body, despite the ways it has changed. I know the safety of him, even if I don't know him as a person anymore. He rests his chin on top of my head. Some part of him is still the boy who gave me my childhood.

And I've missed him so badly.

"We have to stick together now," he says. "We can take care of each other, I promise"

"What about your father? What about the life you're leaving behind? You could get the X drug, be safe, have a normal life…"

Logan shakes his head slowly. "I care more for you than I ever will for him. He's hurt too many people, too many times. After I confronted him I knew…my place is with you. I don't care if it leaves me penniless. These years we've been apart, everything's been wrong. We always took care of one another, Raven. It can be like that again."

It can. Maybe it will. I'm wary. I'm less trusting than he is. He has no reason to doubt anyone or their motives. He'll learn to, when everything falls apart. But if he trusts in me, then maybe this can work. Maybe I can learn to trust him again too. Logan's hands find the side of my face. His thumbs brush away tears I didn't realize were falling.

"You don't need to be scared. You're not alone anymore."

Alone…there's so much he doesn't know. I never told him about my brother, knowing how dangerous it was to admit his existence to anyone, even my best friend. I take a deep breath.

"It's not just me," I tell him, lowering my voice even though there's no one else around. "I have…I have a brother. His name is Jonah. He's weak, and we've kept him hidden away for a long time to protect him, to protect our family. He's everything to me…and I'm all he has, now."

"A brother?" Logan whispers, his eyes wide. No one has siblings and lives to talk about it. This must be a shock to his system, and I know this could get us both into trouble, but it feels good to finally talk to someone about this.

"Does this…does this change things?"

Logan glances at me and firmly shakes his head. He

reaches out for my hands. "I'll help you take care of Jonah. I'll do whatever you need me to. If you want to stay here and stand your ground...we can do that. But it's like you said...we have some options. I can get us the X drug, if that's what you want. I could get us a small place here in the city. Make a life for us. I'll get a job. I'm old enough now, and qualified. we could walk away from this now. Is that what you want?"

This is the same old Logan. The one I recognise and love. Always wanting what's best for us. For me. It's tempting. So tempting to forget that the world is falling apart. That millions will die. I could set myself apart from that. Turn a blind eye to the suffering of others. But if not for Logan, that would be me. I would be just another forgotten soul among the masses. A number, a statistic. And that's why I can't take the offer. I shake my head at him, taking a step back.

"We can't go. If we go, everyone here will die. We'd be letting them down. They'll starve."

Logan's expression is pained. "But you were right, Raven. There's no way we can keep this up for long. I don't have much left in savings. I can't feed all these people on pennies."

He's right. I can understand why he's pushing for us to leave. He's never had to live like I have. He's never known the meaning of having nothing. But if he wants to stay with me, this is the price he'll have to pay. I'm asking a lot, but I'm standing firm.

"I know that. I don't expect you to. We will just have to make do. It's like June says — we have to at least try out some options. Steal. Scrounge. Ration. Grow some food. It's worth a shot." *And I can't face the alternative,* I think to myself.

Logan pauses to give it some thought. But ultimately, I know he'll agree. If he's anything like the boy I knew, he won't leave these people behind. Even if their situation is hopeless.

"Okay. Maybe I could keep a little money aside, just for us. Just in case." He pauses. Smiles. "As long as we're together."

I can't take it any longer. I've missed him too much to hold back. I pull him into another hug. He smells good. Smoke lingers on his jacket, but his skin smells fresh, like soap. I bury my face into him. Letting go doesn't seem like an option.

"I've missed you so much. You have no idea," he mutters. I close my eyes. The ache inside me numbs a little.

"I think I do."

RILEY

The fight starts tomorrow at noon. It's going to be a full house – Lion sold every single ticket, and then some. Every seat will be filled, and there'll be people sitting on the stone stairways too. I don't think I've ever seen such a hyped-up fight. The stands have never been much more than half full in any of my fights. Weirdly, I'm a little jealous. I need to get my priorities straight.

But things are so damn tense in the group. Every meal time, Eagle and Bull sit on opposite ends of the table, eyeing each other up and looking away when they catch each other staring. The usual loud banter has ceased completely. At first, Squid tried to keep us all talking, but after a while, he gave up. No one's in the mood for jokes.

On the plus side, Pup's out of the infirmary. On the downside? We're not talking. I'm too proud to go to her first. She's the one that got mad for no reason. Or no good enough reason. But she's proud too. It's her gutsiest quality. It doesn't help with the awkwardness at meals, though. During the days, I train to keep out of people's way. I figure it'll come in handy even when I leave the Pits. At night, I pretend I can't hear Eagle crying in the dark.

I haven't seen her all day. I expected her to be in the gym.

Bull's been in there most days, though she always leaves when Eagle comes in. Eagle trains at night, Bull by day. But Eagle didn't show up today. I waited. I'd spoken to Bull to say good luck. I wanted to do the same for Eagle. But I looked everywhere and couldn't find her. It was only when I wandered into the arena that I saw her slim figure hunched on a bench in the stands. It's silent out here. Tomorrow, it'll be alive with noise. But for now I can't even hear Eagle's sobs.

I cross the Pit slowly. The sand in the pit is soft and welcoming beneath my feet. I used to love the feel of sand between my toes back when I lived by the sea. It means something different to me now. It means the place where blood is spilled. It means being careful not to slide on it as you run from an opponent. It means life or death. And that's never a happy thought.

My boots clank on the metal benches as I dart up them. Eagle looks up when she hears me. She wipes her eyes on her ragged gray hoodie as I sit next to her. We're quiet for a while, watching as the wind disturbs the sand. The air is gritty with it, and it stings my eyes. Another gust of wind scatters sand on Eagle's face. It's dotted on her lips and face like freckles, until her tears make tracks through it. She's breathing funny, like she's got a cold.

"If I survive this, I'll never watch a Pit fight. Never ever," she says hoarsely.

I nod in understanding. I don't point out that if she wins, she'll likely never come across another fighting pit. It's not going to be in huge demand, after all. Not now. The shift in mood is evident. People are skimping more with their money. The slum dwellers outside the Pits have moved on, only to be replaced by others who are trying to escape from somewhere else. Trouble is, there's nowhere to go. People will realize that soon enough.

"I've never been so scared, Phoenix," Eagle whispers to me. "I get nervous before each fight. Of course I do. But once I go in for the kill, I just close my eyes and let my body go into autopilot. I've never had to fight a friend. Not outside of training."

"It sucks. It really does."

Eagle's lip trembles. She looks like a child right now. It's hard to watch, so I don't. I look back out at the Pit. For once, I'm wishing I was elsewhere. Anywhere else.

"You know, I've been telling myself all week that I can do this. If I just pretend she's someone else." She closes her eyes, a tear dribbling onto her long nose. "I think I could fight one of the others. Tiger or Squid or Pup. You, even. But not her."

"You'd probably say that if you were fighting one of us too."

Eagle shakes her head. "No. It's different with her. I can't...I can't explain."

I can. Eagle's been in love with Bull since the day she met her. They clicked in a way I've never really understood, making gooey eyes at one another twenty-four seven, but never really admitting how they felt. I guess it's a risk falling in love when you could die any day of the week in the Pits. Maybe that's why they kept their distance from one another in that respect.

Eagle has never said anything out loud, of course. We're all friends here, but we keep ourselves to ourselves. We don't share secrets like we're at a rich kid's sleepover. Secrets like that make us weak. So I don't say anything. Eagle would hate for me to know how she truly feels. I can't pretend that I've ever felt anything like romantic love before, and I've long been sure that I never will, but I know, from what people have told me, that it hurts.

And now I see why.

"If I get out of here...I don't think I'll be able to live with myself."

"You will. You'll get through it. It won't be easy, but you'll be alive. You'll hurt, but you'll survive."

Eagle sniffs. Her fingers shakily plait a thick hunk of hair. "I'm not convinced. I'm not like you. I don't take everything in my stride. Things affect me more."

"Why do people keep saying that? You think I don't get hurt?"

"That's not what I said. I know you get hurt. But you hurt back. And then you get back on your feet. You fight."

Eagle's eyes are glistening as she looks at me. I feel patronized, but I keep my mouth shut. She watches me with an odd look in her eyes, like she feels protective of me. I get that a lot from the older kids here. I guess they see me as a child, even though I grew out of that a long time ago.

"You're so young, Riley. At your age, I was still clinging to my mother."

I sniff. "Yeah? Well I haven't got one. I had to pave my own way. What do people expect me to do? Keel over?"

Eagle stands up, brushing sand off herself. "Yes, Riley. That's what the rest of us would do."

I grab Eagle's arm to stop her moving away. "No. No you wouldn't. You haven't. When you're close to death, you cling on to life with whatever you've got left. When you're starving on the street, you do what it damn takes to get that next meal. And tomorrow, in the Pit, you'll do the same. And then after? If you win? You'll do the same." I shake my head at Eagle. "Don't be a damn idiot. You're here because you're a fighter. Don't forget that."

Eagle looks away. "I don't want to be a fighter anymore."

For some reason, that comment chills me right to my very core.

The dorm is quiet as we get ready for bed. Bull sits on her bed, staring into space. Pup tried to get her to change into her night clothes, but she won't budge. Bull's built like a mountain anyway. Not one of us can force her to do something she doesn't want to.

I think Eagle must be thinking the same. She's been staring at Bull for the past ten minutes. I can only imagine what's going through her brain. It's a toughie. But once again, I'm just glad it isn't me.

But I have other things to worry about. Like how to claim

my money and slip away unnoticed. Since agreeing to go with Squid, he's asked Pup and Tiger along too. I'm sure he'll ask whoever survives the fight to join him as well. So at least he won't be on his own.

I've changed my mind a million times this week, but I've decided it's best that I don't go with them. If I leave now, I won't know whether they live or die. If I stay with them, I'll know the second they're in danger. I'll know every time they're hurting. I'll know if they die. And I don't want that. I've watched it happen to too many people I love. Now that I have the choice, I choose not to let that happen to me. Even if it means being alone.

I fold my map up carefully and put it in my backpack. I need to be ready to go after the fight. Tiger's packed too, and is helping Pup with her bag. Squid's not prepared yet, as usual. He's calmer than all of us, as always. It calms me a little, too.

I'll miss him when I go.

Squid comes and sits beside me on my bed and I rest my head against his shoulder. Neither of us say anything. I know if I talk now, I'll cry. And I don't cry. I just don't. I can't. Not my style. I don't do it even when I really want to.

Eagle stands suddenly and crosses the room. Bull looks up and backs away, shuffling further on to her bed. Eagle stands over her, eyes wet. She puts her hand on Bull's cheek. She's too surprised to move away. Eagle's thumb moves under Bull's eye to wipe away a tear.

"I'm not going to kill you," she whispers. Squid squeezes my hand, and I furrow my brow. Does she mean she'll let Bull kill her? But she doesn't explain herself. She just crosses the room again and gets into her bed. Tiger stands to go over to Eagle, but Pup catches his eye and shakes her head. Bull trembles in her bed, not knowing what to say or do. Everyone stays in silence for a long while. Squid gets up, ruffling my hair before retreating to his own bed.

And for the first time since Bull and Eagle were chosen, for some reason, I feel fear.

I don't sleep. Not until late in the night. And when I finally fall asleep, I wake to screaming. I'm on my feet in seconds, my hand on the knife I keep by my bedside. I blink through bleary eyes. Bull's standing by Eagle's bedside, clutching her hand and sobbing.

The others are stirring too. I rush to Eagle's bedside. Her eyes are open, but unseeing. Her skin is white and pasty. I click my fingers in front of her eyes desperately. She doesn't blink. I grab her shoulders and shake.

"Stop it! Leave her in peace!" Bull sobs. I stagger away from the bed. I can't breathe. There's a sharp pain in my heart. A friend is dead. But the second stab to my heart hurts even more. Because I'm realizing something pretty damn fast.

If she's dead, what does it mean for the rest of us?

Lion bursts into the room. She spots Eagle and stops dead.

"Is she?" she dares ask. I feel two hands on my shoulder. Tiger and Squid. I think they're the only thing keeping me standing.

This wasn't supposed to happen.

Lion shoves Bull aside and checks Eagle's pulse. She fishes under her bed. She produces a bottle of bleach. Pup gasps. I retch, turning away. This can't be happening. It can't.

Lion straightens up, brushing invisible dirt from her nightshirt. She shakes her head. "One of you will replace her."

We don't have any choice. As Bull sobs in the background, we form a circle. Somehow, as Lion puts our names on slips of paper and shuffles them in her pocket, I know. I know as she delves her hand into her pocket exactly who she'll pick.

Her eyes meet mine.

I'm fighting Bull in the Pit.

KARISSA

Training is monotonous. Almost dull. My mind is elsewhere and has been all week. I'm still wondering what the hell happened to me during the Pain Endurance class. Whatever it was, it hasn't happened again.

I think about the white room day and night. Sometimes, I dream about it. I dream about getting close to the black blanket, and whatever's underneath it. Sometimes, I think I'll see what's under there. Sometimes I get so close to touching the blanket, I can almost feel it on my fingertips. But then I wake and I'm left even more confused than before.

It shouldn't be bothering me so much. Everything's going well for me. Since Pain Endurance, I've improved in all of my classes. I've been beating all of my own personal times and scores. I've been top of the class in everything. My team has been watching me like I'm some kind of superhero. Marcia hangs off of my every word. Minnie twirls her hair when I talk, lips pouted. Zach and Ronan laugh at my jokes. Inevitably, Elliott hates me more than ever. But I can't find it in me to care. I know even with the added attention, I won't be chosen as Team Leader. So it seems irrelevant. Certainly not as important as solving the mysteries of last week.

I'm walking to class in a daze. Marcia is chatting in my ear.

I have no idea what she's talking about, I'm too distracted. But now something catches my eye. I spot Captain Strauss up ahead, herding students away from the classrooms. I stop dead, frowning. She approaches us, fixating her black eyes on me.

"Change of plans, Team Nine. To the hall, please," she says. Then she leaves without another word.

"What's going on?" Marcia says. I don't say anything, but I have a feeling this is it. This is the moment we'll vote for our Team Leader.

I've not even thought about who I'll vote for. Zach seems like the best choice to me. Not that it matters what I think when I already know what the others are planning to do. I know what the result will be. Elliott's going to win. This week alone won't be enough to sway the others or their vote. And that means game over for me.

In the hall, all twelve teams are gathered at their usual tables. Minnie slides into the seat next to me. Ronan and Zach are opposite, and Elliott's lumped on the end of the bench with Marcia. Captain Strauss stands on her podium at the front of the hall, on which is her control panel. It controls all of our wristwatches, as well as the counting of the electronic voting system. She calls for our attention, and the hall falls silent. She catches my eye looking smug, as though to say *see what respect can do?*

"Today is the day to choose your Team Captains. I want you all to think carefully before you choose, and don't base your vote on what everyone else in the team wants. I want your honest opinion on who is fit to lead. In the event of a tie within a team, I will choose the Captain, and the person who tied for first place will become the Second. However, if the vote is unanimous, the Captain will be able to select their own Second. It goes without saying really, but again, I ask you to choose wisely. These Team Leaders are for life."

I look at table seven, where Adelaide sits tall, her teammates looking at her in admiration. I feel my shoulders sag. I know I won't win this. It'll take more than one admirable incident and a week of success to make me Team Captain.

But Captain Strauss isn't finished.

"However. It has come to my attention that several teams among you are rule-breaking. I am aware that several members have been breaking curfew, stealing from kitchens, and keeping unauthorized weaponry on their presence. This is unacceptable. I don't know why any of you believed you could break the rules and get away with it, but now, you will face the consequences. The following teams will have the privilege to vote revoked based on the crimes, and I will be choosing their captains. Team Three. Team Four." Captain Strauss pauses. Her eyes drift to my table. "Team Nine."

Elliott stands, slamming his hand against the table. "You can't do that!"

Captain Strauss purses her lips, and presses a button on her control panel. Elliott cries out as his wristwatch electrifies, sending a bolt of energy and pain through his body. He has the sense to slump back into his seat and remain silent in his humiliation.

"I can do that, Soldier Gray. And in fact, you are one of the reasons that your team is having their vote revoked. If you would like me to list the offenses you have committed to humiliate you further, please speak up again."

Elliott glares at his own feet, silent in fury. Zach slams his elbow into Elliott's stomach in annoyance, folding his big arms over his chest. The whole team is glaring at him, but my eyes are on Captain Strauss. I know what is coming.

She's going to pick me.

While the others cast their votes, we're sent back to our classrooms. But the trainer hasn't arrived, so I watch the others confront Elliott.

"You dumbass!" Minerva hisses. "Breaking curfew? You're lucky she didn't punish you more…"

"And now we don't even get to vote?" Zach huffs.

"Well, at least we know you won't get picked," Minerva hisses at Elliott. I watch him register the insult. Hurt flickers across his face, before it hardens to stone.

"She said I was one of the reasons," he says quietly. "Stealing from the kitchens...does that sound familiar, Minnie?" Glaring eyes turn to her and she blushes, her dark eyebrows knitting together as she glares back defensively.

Elliott whips around to look at Ronan. "Unauthorized weaponry? I wonder who that could be..."

My mouth falls open in shock and Ronan blushes, shrinking away. "I didn't know you knew about that."

"I know everything about every single one of you," Elliott hisses. He circles us all, like we're his prey.

"Yeah?" Zach snarls. "Well now that you're crossed off as Team Leader, maybe you should know this – we can't stand you. You've bullied us into submission, and we've let it happen. We all thought it was too late to do something about you, so we took precautions. Ronan stole that knife to protect himself from *you*."

Zach squares up to Elliott and jabs a finger into his chest. "You're toxic. But you've got nothing now. We've had our right to vote taken away. But at least now we'll get a leader worthy of us."

His speech sends the group into stunned silence. I stare at Elliott. For the first time in what seems like a lifetime, he looks upset. Frightened. It reminds me that like us, he has a heart. A soul. Even if he buries it deep. Zach is glaring at him, and Ronan has a hand on his shoulder, holding him back. Minnie's smirk has slipped and she's biting her nails. Marcia's standing close behind me. Like I'm her shield. Like she trusts that I'll keep her safe if a fight starts. My heart's thumping. She's starting to trust me.

"There's nothing we can do now," Marcia squeaks from behind me.

"That's right, Marcia. The decision has been made."

We all turn to see Captain Strauss standing at the door to the gym. We salute her obediently – even Elliott – and she nods, smiling.

"It's good to see that you've not run completely amok,"

she says. She nods to me. "Soldier Karissa Gray. I choose you as Team Captain."

I hear some muttering behind me, but a sharp look from Captain Strauss silences whoever it is. She looks back at me.

"I expect you at a meeting at five o'clock to further discuss your duties and your choice of Second. I want to give you time so that you select them carefully."

I salute dutifully. "I hope to do you proud, Captain."

She nods to me, taking a second to survey the shocked faces of my teammates. She smirks. I think she's proud of the chaos she's caused. "I don't doubt that you will. I wish you luck."

Then Captain Strauss leaves and I'm left with the remains of a team that's just fallen apart. I stare at them all. They're watching me, expectant.

Because now, whether I like it or not, they answer to me.

RILEY

I stand in front of the dirty mirror. An ugly child with puffed up eyes stares back. I have two minutes to cry before people will start to question where I am. two minutes to fill the shoes of a winner.

Mere hours until the fight. I'm not ready for this. I'm not ready to face a friend in the Pit. But I'm not ready to die either. Everything I said to Eagle is true – I know that once I'm out there, fighting for my life, I'll be a machine. I'll be able to kill her.

I'm going to kill her.

If I'm going to be a monster one last time, I may as well look the part. I've already got the gruesome battle scars etched into my flesh. I've already got the crooked teeth and flushed face. Now, all I have to deal with is my hair.

I guess I don't really need my hair. I'm not a vain person. But I'll miss it. It's my favorite feature. It's long and tangled, but it's the color of fire and anger and I think that suits me just fine. But I've got to eliminate any weakness. This ain't just any fight. This is a pro versus a pro. I've got to be at my best. It'll only get in the way.

I let myself cry as I hack at my hair with my knife. It falls to the floor in orange tendrils. I hack and hack until all I'm left with is an orange fuzz on the top of my head. I run my hand over it. In some ways, I like it.

But I don't look like myself. And that's good. I have to give up Riley today and give in to the stranger I become each time I kill.

I can hear the crowd from in here. Their cries of excitement fill the air. There have been a couple of small fights to warm them up. In several minutes, it'll be my turn.

Squid, Pup and Tiger have been sitting with me all morning. None of us have said much, but Squid has left the room several times. I heard him crying in the corridor. It's a little offensive, really.

He thinks I'm going to lose.

So far, I've managed to forget that it's Bull I'll be facing. But now, it's dawning on me. I'll walk out into the arena and she'll be standing there. Ready to try and kill me. The girl who taught me how to plait hair. The girl whose laugh is so loud, it turns every damn head in the room. That girl will have a knife in her hand today. That knife has my name on it.

I stare ahead of me. In front of me, there's a set of large wooden doors. I've walked through them a thousand times. On the other side is the sandy Pit and the crowd and the enemy. The enemy today is Bull. And that's something I'll just have to swallow.

I've said goodbye to this place. To the warm bed and the shower and the hot food that lines my belly. But I'm not going to say goodbye to my friends. Because there's no way I'm dying today. Even if I have to sell my soul to the damn Devil.

The double doors open and the cheering gets louder. The crowd is waiting for me. The man at the door ushers me forwards. I feel Pup grapple for my hand as I stand, trying to hold me back but I brush her away.

"Don't. Don't say anything."

"But I need you to know that I'm-"

"It can wait. I ain't dying," I snap. Then I walk out of the waiting room. It'll be over soon. One hour from now, I'll be the ultimate champion. I may have to carry that burden for the rest of my life, but at least I'll be alive. That's what I have to focus on now.

It's midday. Sunny. Doesn't seem very fitting for the mood. My ears hurt from the cheering in the crowd. I feel sand smushing beneath my boots as I walk. I'll be one of the last to walk out here. Tomorrow, this place will be abandoned. I come to a stop in the middle of the Pit and everyone cheers for my presence.

I can't see Bull yet. I stare at the tunnel where she'll emerge from. The doors are open, but she's not made an appearance yet. I squint into the darkness of the tunnel. The crowd is getting impatient. Their calls are getting louder. My heart is giving my chest a good pounding. Where the hell is she?

Two men drag Bull into the tunnel. She kicks out at them. Her nose is dribbling. The men throw her down in the sand and rush back to the doors, shutting them fast. No turning back now. Bull scrabbles to her feet, throwing herself at the door. The crowd falls quiet as they watch Bull's desperate attempt to escape. Everyone can hear her crying now. I have to do something to get her moving, to remind her to fight for her life. I can't fight her like this. I'm not taking down an injured animal.

And no one can walk away until someone dies.

"What are you waiting for?" I yell at her, raising my arms, challenging her. "Come get me."

The crowd cheers, and Bull turns slowly. Her face is screwed up in rage. At me. At her predicament. At the lot we've been given in life. And I'm angry too. But I stay calm. I have to if I want to live.

Bull sets off at a run, which sends the crowd crazy. She enters the pit, sand flying up behind her feet. I prep myself, a hand on my knife. Bull launches herself at me and her body slams into mine. We tumble to the floor. Adrenaline kicks in. I stab at her face. She deflects me, pinning my arm down.

She whacks me and I feel my jaw crack. The crowd love it. Me? Not so much.

She doesn't stop. She punches over and over. My nose gives in, blood flowing into my open mouth as I cry out. I dodge one punch only to be met by another. Bull's eyes are filled with all sorts of crazy. She's not herself. She's got into a frenzy. The way we all do.

I need to do the same.

I manage to slam my knee into Bull's stomach. She recoils. I have a few seconds to get my act together. I tumble sideways. Bull's much bigger than me, but as she registers the pain in her stomach, I manage to knock her over. I kneel over her, finally dominant. Droplets of my blood shower her face. I stab, aiming for her neck, trying to end it quickly. But she misdirects me and my knife lodges in her upper arm. She winces and swats at me with her huge hands, forcing me to retreat backwards.

I clamber to my feet, much to the crowd's approval. I let out a battle cry and charge at Bull as she regains her footing. She grabs my wrist to stop me stabbing her face. Her knife skims my side. It rips my shirt, nicks my skin. She stabs again and I manage to dodge. Then I feel the searing pain in my upper leg. Her knife is buried deep.

I buckle and fall to the floor. I stab desperately at Bull's legs, but dark stars cloud my eyes. I yank Bull's knife out of my leg and yelp, falling back as my vision goes completely black. Bull tries to wrestle her knife from my grip, her knee jabbing in my wound. The pain consumes me and I lose my grip. Before I know it, I have no weapon and she has two.

Now I know how it feels to be the prey. I limp away as fast as I can, trying to clear the cloud in my head. I need a clear mind. But I feel a knife sink into my shoulder, connecting with bone. I cry out in chorus with the crowd's cheers. The pain is so intense that I feel like I might throw up.

I should give in.

No. That's not me. I just have to up my game. I don't try

to remove the knife. I just turn to face Bull, circling her. She's breathless, matching my steps. When she darts at me, I'm ready. I grab her wrist as she stabs. Our shoulders connect as she tries to throw me down, but I stand firm. My knee drives into her stomach. Once. Twice. I sink my teeth into her shoulder. My jaw jars as she yowls and her shoulder butts into my teeth, practically rattling them in my mouth, but I hold firm. She wants to play dirty? I can do that. I taste blood. She slashes at my face, slicing me up, but I barely feel it. I'm too damn pumped. I grab her wrist and twist her arm around. The knife clatters to the floor. And finally, the ball is in my court. I snatch it up and hobble away. I need a few seconds to figure out my plan.

I whip back to look at Bull. I've seen the look she wears once before – when a rabid dog went crazy in the slums and bit a man's hand off. It's a feral look. Animalistic. Crazy. Desperate. She stares me down, trying to look tough. But all I feel is sad. Somehow, I feel like she wants to win more than me. But I tell myself that I have more left to live for. She's lost everything. While I sat with my friends before the fight, she sat alone, the ghost of her best friend fresh in her mind. I grip the knife with sweaty hands. This is my fight to win. I have to win. I've made it this far. I'll make it to the end.

I stagger towards her. She's not wounded, but I have a chance now. I have a knife. She could crush my windpipe with her bare hands, but I ignore that. It's time to end this with my signature move. I just have to be positioned right.

I'm close enough. Bull stomps towards me, her boots creating sandstorms and earthquakes. Tears sting my eyes. I ready my knife.

"I'm sorry it's ending this way," I whisper, feeling the gurgle of fresh blood in my throat. I close my eyes. I know where to aim anyway.

Then I throw the knife.

I hear the crowd gasp. For a moment, I wonder if I missed. But then I feel the tremor beneath my feet as Bull hits the floor. I feel the sand shockwave over my ankles and feet. When I open my eyes, Bull lies, eyes open, hands on her throat. The knife sticks out from between her fingers. I feel the tears come before I can try and stop them.

The crowd is wild. I've got a standing ovation. The underdog has won, and they're loving it. I stumble over to her. The adrenaline is dying down. Reality hits. I can feel the blade in my back. The one in my heart. I fall to my knees by Bull. Her eyes find me, and she tries to speak.

"Ri…ley…"

I shake my head, my throat closing up. I want to speak, to tell her I'm sorry, but I can't. I pull her head onto my lap. Press my palm to her sweaty head. She whimpers, and I hush her. I feel like a mother. But I'm a child. And there's no one here to hold me.

I feel it when she dies. Her eyes are locked on mine as the life goes out of her. I feel the sag of tense muscles. Her body gives in. And the cheers don't stop. They roar around my ears. I stare around with blurred eyes.

"What's wrong with you all?" I cry out. "She was my friend!"

They don't hear me. They're cheering too loud. And suddenly, my body wants to give in too. So I let it. I give into the pain. It's almost a relief when the black stars cloud my eyes again and I fade.

EPILOGUE

Captain Strauss had eyes everywhere. Long before Ireland had split from the rest of the United Kingdom, it had been infested with cameras everywhere; outside stores, on the streets, inside every bank, school and institution. Now, she used them to watch as chaos reigned the streets of London from the safety of the Irish Institute.

Among the crowd, she saw her gray jumpsuiters, clawing their way through the citizens, manic after so long cooped up in their cages. They were Phase One, a way to take out the true dregs of society, made into reckless zombies by a former strain of the X drug. *A damn shame to waste so many lives on failed experiments,* she thought, *but a necessity.* Without trialing the twenty-three drugs that came before the X drug, she never would have reached the dizzy heights she'd come to know. Now, she had control. Now, she was clearing the way for her true prodigies.

Their time was coming. A time when the young lives she'd shaped would truly thrive. Soon, the soldiers she had raised would take to the streets of Britain and tear it apart. The world she envisioned would only work if they were able to break it down first and then build it up from the ashes. Thanks to the X drug, the fruits of her labor, they would start anew on the barren lands. They would repopulate with better human beings. They would wipe out the scum that had plagued the country she had once known as a child, and rise above. It made her heart swell with pride just to think about what was to come.

She could see the beginnings of it all unfolding. Since Alistair Fairfax had made his announcement, panic had ensued. That was good. Panic was what she needed to flush out the rats from the sewers to the streets. That's how they would identify their targets. And once the purge was complete, her hard work would finally mean something. The children she had raised to be warriors would finally understand what all their training was for.

And they would see the dawn of a new world.

It was time to set the wheels in motion for the future. Captain Strauss dialed the number of Alistair Fairfax, and within two rings, she had made it through to the British Parliament.

"Good evening, Prime Minister. Are you ready to initiate Phase Two?"

TO BE CONTINUED…

ABOUT THE AUTHOR

HAYLEY ANDERTON is a full time ghostwriter and the author of the YA LGBT romance novel, Double Bluff. She is also the co-author of the Kindle Unlimited series, Apocalypse. When she's not writing she loves to bake and hang out with fluffy friends. For editing services and business enquiries, she can be contacted at hayleyandertonbusiness@gmail.com.

Instagram: @hayley_a_writes
Twitter: @handerton96
Wattpad: @hazzer123

If you enjoyed this novel, please consider reviewing it on Amazon and Goodreads! Reviews can make or break an indie author's career, so any thoughts you have are much appreciated!

Printed in Great Britain
by Amazon

13469177R00066